# Welcome Home

## Hearts & Home Book 1

## Bonnie Phelps

Lilac Lace Press

## DEDICATION

To my amazing husband for all of his support and for introducing me to the meaning of true romance! To my daughters for all their encouragement and support. To all the amazing entrepreneurial women who fearlessly tackle what others do not think possible and fill the world with their energy.

# Contents

# Chapter One

JESSICA WINTERS, 'JESS' TO everyone, cursed when a sharp pain shot up her leg. She'd banged her shin as she stepped over one of the cross-piece boards tacked to the framing of the new home under construction. What was wrong with her today? She definitely needed more caffeine and to keep her mind on business. Stupid to let her dad get under her skin... again.

Ever since his construction business folded, life had taken a nose dive. Each year, he'd withdrawn a little more, until now, seventeen years later, he was bitter and indifferent. Every chance he got, he let her know she'd never make a go of it in construction. It hadn't been easy, and she learned the hard way to be careful who she trusted, but so far she'd done a good job of proving him wrong.

Narrowing her eyes against the throbbing in her shin, she wished she could bend down and rub the sore spot. But as one of the few female general contractors in the Sacramento California area, she had to appear tough. Any sign of weakness and Uniquely Yours, Construction and Design—the all-female company she and four of her friends owned and operated—and they could easily lose potential clients to their male competitors. As a petite, blue-eyed blonde, Jess didn't fit the hard-nosed image in this male-dominated industry.

The partners weren't about to let the success of their company hinge on the vagaries of public perception so they'd saved every penny they could spare. Using that seed money, they started buying homes in need of tender loving care, fixing them up, and then reselling them. Flipping homes had become their primary revenue stream, but they still took on remodeling or new construction projects. Versatility was key. No matter what the job, their goal remained the same—to create the perfect home so the people who lived there felt comfortable laughing, loving, and dreaming.

And wasn't that hope for her clients exactly what she wanted for herself? To build a place where she could thrive? Where she felt respected and loved? Her lips softened. She also longed for a partner who would make her secret romantic heart beat faster. A man who'd always have her back as they built a home and a family together. Now in her early thirties, she wondered if that man would ever appear.

Sighing, she glanced down and kept moving, flicking between the pages on the clipboard she carried. That was, until she came to an abrupt halt against a solid wall of masculine chest. Cursing again and inhaling deeply, she got a lungful of pure man. Jess glared at the immovable object blocking her path. An odd zing of attraction bounced around her like an annoying fly. Mentally she swatted it away and stood her ground under his assessing gaze.

"Ya lost pal? This is private property." Jess inched her hardhat higher on her forehead and tapped her pen against her clipboard. Darkly handsome, broody eyes, scruff on his jaw, dark hair that skimmed his collar—the kind of man who wasn't on her agenda today and maybe ever.

"Nope. Told to come here before seven and meet a guy named Jess."

His low, husky voice wrapped around her like her favorite sweater. She frowned and heard her friend Victoria's voice in her head nagging her to lighten up. '*Laugh lines age much better than frown lines.*' The thought almost made her smile. "We'll you've found her." Jess arched one brow. "What can I do for you?" She hated having to act tough, but if she didn't, people tended to walk all over her.

"Understand you're hiring." The stranger didn't fidget or act nervous in any way. Simply stood quietly and waited. He also hadn't shown surprise that Jess was a she and not a he.

"Do you have any experience in construction?" She gazed into blue eyes that reminded her of rain clouds.

"No Ma'am, but I hear you hire unskilled labor..." He looked at the ground and then up, refocusing his intense gaze on her. "I could use the work. I'm willing to do whatever needs doing."

Jess examined the stranger. Gave herself time to gauge his suitability. Reserved. Self-contained. She wasn't picking up any bad vibes, and she had a soft spot for those down on their luck. He wasn't a kid. She placed his age around mid-thirty. Kind of late to get into construction. "Okay, I'll give you a chance. What you do with it is up to you. You'll be rotated where we need you. I assume you have reliable transportation?"

He angled his head towards a beat-up Chevy truck at the curb. "It's old, but it gets me where I need to go."

Jess retrieved a business card from her pocket. "Go to this address and talk to Kaitlin Connors, our business manager. She'll have you fill out our paperwork, give you a list of tools you'll need, and assign you to a work site for tomorrow." She watched a shadow pass over his face.

"Look, if you're short on cash, let Kaitlin know. We do have some loaner tool belts and tools you can check out until you can purchase your own."

"That would be much appreciated."

Jess stuck out her hand. "And you are?"

"Devin. Devin Miller." He accepted her hand and a tingle raced up her arm. That was unexpected.

Jess pulled her hand back as discreetly as possible. A truck door slammed, and she turned toward the sound. The interruption provided an excuse to dismiss this disquieting man and focus on the reason she was here. She smiled as she watched her blue team foreman hurry toward her. Bill Harriman, built like a refrigerator with a beer belly, smoothed down what was left of his ginger hair before he plunked his hardhat on his head.

"Sorry I'm late. There was a wreck on the interstate."

"No problem. Just got here myself." Jess watched his gaze flick to the man at her side. "Bill, meet Devin. He just hired on as a new floater and is leaving to fill out the paperwork."

The two men exchanged a hand shake. With a nod to her, Devin strode toward his truck.

After Devin had driven off, Bill asked, "Another stray?"

Jess scowled at her foreman. "He needed a job, and in this tight labor market, I take anyone who looks like they have potential."

Bill stepped back and held up his hands in surrender. "No judgement."

She willed herself to relax and then smiled at Bill. "I know. I'm a softie. He seemed grateful for the chance." She shrugged. "What can I say? I'll assign him to my crew for the first week to see how he does and then hand him over to you to finish his training."

"If he shows any promise, you can count on me to bring him along."

She didn't miss the quick grin he tried to hide. "I know you will." Returning his grin, she added, "Most of my hunches have paid off, and by giving folks a chance, they tend to be pretty loyal."

"Can't fault your instincts. You've put together a top notch crew."

She shrugged, secretly basking in Bill's praise. "He seemed like a good risk." She clapped him on the back as they moved forward into the shell of the building. "Where are we with this project?" Her head swiveled as she scrutinized the work. Clear of debris. Everything looked solid. Permits clearly visible.

"You got my text that the inspector signed off on the framing permit yesterday?"

Jess nodded.

"Kaitlin said the sheathing and house wrap materials will be delivered..." he glanced at his watch, "any time now. I've got my crew scheduled to arrive in about thirty minutes. We'll have this house buttoned up and ready for us to install the windows and exterior doors in the next few days. Roofers are scheduled for next week."

"Any issues I need to know about?" Jess finished making notes and closed the clipboard.

"One of the crew said he was approached by BL Construction to come work for them, but he turned them down." He glanced toward the beeping sound of a large truck backing up to the site. "Here's our supplies... Anyway I just thought you should know."

"Thanks Bill. Poaching good employees is a fact of life in this business." Her lips thinned, and she adjusted her hardhat. Figured it was Brendon's outfit trying to poach. Sleazy bastard. "I'm off to touch base with Rollo and his crew, then meet my crew to start demo on the new Jackson Street flip." She wanted to pinch herself. They had three projects running simultaneously and another property closing in two weeks. A dream come true.

"Rollo said you had to replace the heating and air system on his job. Slowed things up a bit, plus an unexpected expense." Bill tugged his jeans over his belly and back up to his waist. "Tough break. Shame you couldn't repair it."

"Yeah, but I haven't cut corners yet, and I'm not about to start now. Uniquely Yours means quality. Our reputation is everything." She tilted her head and glanced at Bill. "I may pull a carpenter from here next week to keep Rollo's project on schedule. Got cabinets and trim work slated for then, and his crew needs to be ready to start on the new flip in a month."

"Whatever you need."

"You want us to unload this in the garage?" The delivery man shouted.

"Be right there," Bill shouted back.

"Go take care of business." Jess set off toward her truck. "Holler if you need anything," she called over her shoulder. When she reached her truck, she paused to admire the new logo emblazoned on the door of her new Ford F-350. They'd had the vinyl wrap attached yesterday to all their vehicles.

She traced a finger over the lettering, relishing the thrill. Proof of their progress. The five friends had come a long way since starting their business fresh out of college six years ago. They hadn't looked back since purchasing their first house to flip three years ago. Once the current projects in the pipeline closed escrow, they'd be in a position to purchase a piece of land and build their dream offices—that is, once they found it. They'd been looking for a while, but nothing suitable had turned up. Settling herself into the driver's seat, she set her hardhat on the seat beside her, and focused on the tasks ahead.

DEVIN MILLER PARKED IN front of the Uniquely Yours office located in one of the area's nondescript business parks. He studied the long, one story structure in front of him. Built of concrete blocks and painted light tan, it was sturdy and functional but not what he'd envisioned. Their office space was simply one of a long row of glass-fronted suites paired with dark brown roll-up doors off to the side of each unit. He'd thought a company touting itself as one that *builds homes where dreams are made—not just places to live*—would want to greet customers someplace more unusual. But then again, who was he to say appearances meant anything.

Judging wasn't the reason he'd returned to his hometown. Right now he should celebrate that his luck may finally have changed for the better. He'd landed a job with the firm he'd set his sights on. It put him in the path of a woman he'd wanted to meet—a woman who might hold the key to obtaining the information he needed to make things right. At least it was a starting point.

Devin grinned. She did have an attitude. He'd seen the flash of irritation when he said he was looking for a *guy* named Jess, but she'd covered well. Figured she got that a lot. Must be tough running a construction company as a female—especially a petite blonde with the kind of curves that made men's fantasies run wild. She'd looked so darn cute acting all tough. It hadn't been easy keeping his expression neutral when the sparks flying between them were hotter than a tree branch hitting a transformer. He'd watched her try and hide the attraction.

The sigh rose from his diaphragm and seeped out his mouth like a deflating tire—one slow hiss. Until he finished what he'd set out to do, a relationship wasn't part of his plan. Not that he'd ever been much of a planner. Instead, he'd always reacted to the circumstances life threw his way... and left a path littered with bad decisions. He'd come a long way toward cleaning up his life and dealing with his addiction to prescription drugs, but recovery was a daily battle. His goal was to make amends by bringing justice to the people his father had wronged—starting with Jess' dad. Everything else took second place.

Opening his glove compartment, he fished out a manila envelope containing the documents he might need to fill out his application. He stared down at the paperwork in his lap and smoothed a few creases in it with his thumbs. This step represented a new life. A chance to prove he wasn't his past. He wanted to unload the guilt that had plagued him since he was a teen and to hit the restart button.

He eased out of the truck, cringing when the hinges squeaked. Time for a little WD-40. No sense giving people the impression he couldn't take care of himself or his property.

A middle-aged woman dressed in slacks and a sweater set greeted him at the front counter.

"I'm here to see Kaitlin Connors. I think she's expecting me." Devin held the envelope in one hand at his side brushing it against his thigh. He tucked his other hand in his jeans pocket and waited.

"Yes, she is. She'll be right out. Would you like to take a seat?" She indicated several small, padded chairs against the wall.

He nodded and took a seat. Leaning forward with his elbows resting on his knees, he skimmed through the documents to make sure everything was there—birth certificate, social security card, references from the few people he knew in the area, bank statement, lease agreement. A discreet cough brought his head up.

A thirty-something woman with long auburn hair, hazel eyes, and the most welcoming smile he'd ever seen stood in front of him. Devin got to his feet, and she extended her hand. It felt odd meeting a woman who was only a couple inches shorter than he was.

"Hello Mr. Miller, I'm Kaitlin. Please follow me to my office." She motioned for him to walk beside her down the short hallway. "Did you have any trouble finding our offices?"

"No ma'am."

"Good to hear. This complex can seem like a rabbit warren, and all the spaces look the same." She opened the door at the end of the hall and ushered him inside her spacious office. "Please take a seat." She lowered herself into her chair and pulled a file folder in front of her. "I understand you're new to the area. What brought you to Sacramento?"

"Not exactly new. I was born here." A taste like sour milk coated his tongue. He didn't like talking about his past and dodged questions whenever he could. "Moved away." He shrugged. "Decided I wanted to get back to my roots."

"Well then, welcome back." She pulled several forms from the folder and slid each one in front of him as she spoke. "This is the employment application, federal and state tax withholding forms, agreement for random drug testing, I-9 to document your eligibility to work in the U.S., a list of tools you need to provide, and a tool lending agreement..." Kaitlin paused, and he noticed the kindness in her eyes. "Jess said you might need to borrow for a while." She set a pen on top of the paperwork. "I'll take you to our conference room so you can fill all this out. Just come knock on my door when you're finished."

He glanced around the room, and his eyes lighted on a child's toy chest, small table, and chair in the corner.

"I have a four-year-old son who sometimes comes to work with me." Her voice simmered with mother's love—not a sound he'd heard as a child but had heard it in other women's voices. "He likes his own work space when he's here. Makes him feel grown up."

"He's a lucky boy." She smiled at him again but this time it was tinged with sadness. He'd like to ask, but if he pried, that opened the door to questions about him.

It took the better part of an hour to complete all the paperwork. He put the pen down and flexed his fingers. Whatever happened to the old handshake? He gathered everything, walked back to Kaitlin's office, and tapped on the door.

"Come in." She motioned toward a chair and reached out her hand for the forms. He watched her scan the information and pause before setting the forms on her desk. "This is your address?"

Ice formed around his heart. "Is that a problem?"

"No, not at all." Her eyes held nothing but understanding. "How long have you been sober?"

"Two years." He swallowed to get moisture back in his mouth. "How did you know?"

"I had a friend who was part of their program for several years. He's out on his own now and doing well. Homes for Addicts is an amazing organization." She went back to scanning his documents. When she finished, she said, "I'll need to make a copy of your driver's license and social security card."

He pulled his license from his wallet and handed both documents to her. "Will my past make a difference?"

"No, as long as your drug tests come back clean, we're fine."

Devin cleared his throat. "Is this something your partners need to know? I'm still getting used to who I am now." He felt like a drowning man every time he admitted to his former addiction. Would the telling ever get easy?

"I'm in charge of HR, so what you tell me is confidential." She swiveled her chair and set his documents on the copier. When finished, she tucked the copies into a file folder and returned the originals. "I know it's hard to talk about your addiction, but know that when you're ready to share, no one here is going to judge you."

He released the breath he'd been holding. "I appreciate that."

She opened a document on her computer, typed in some information, and printed it out. "This is where you'll work tomorrow. Be there by 7:00AM. You'll report to Jess for the first week." She slid the paper across the desk and stood. "I'll walk you out."

When they reached the lobby, she pointed to a stack of tools against the wall. "Those are yours to use for now. Until you get a locking tool box for your truck, I suggest you bring them inside each night." She extended her hand. "Good luck, and welcome to Uniquely Yours."

After he loaded everything into his truck, Devin sat for a moment behind the wheel sorting through his conflicting emotions. Relief that he'd managed to keep his secret. Guilt and shame that he didn't want anyone to know who his father was. Uncertainty about whether or not he was even doing the right thing.

Resolve settled over him. Yes, he was.

For the first time since crawling out of the hole he'd put himself in, the weight pushing against his lungs eased enough to allow for a deep breath. The fresh oxygen felt great. Sadly, keeping secrets wasn't part of his twelve steps, but making amends was. Knowing his father, Devin had no intention of underestimating his reaction if he discovered someone was trying to bring his past misdeeds to light. He doubted it would be pretty. The fewer people who knew what Devin was up to, the less chance word would filter back to his dad. A slow acid burn worked its way up his esophagus. He'd just have to keep his secrets a little longer.

# Chapter Two

JESS POURED HERSELF A cup of coffee and plucked a fresh-baked blueberry muffin off the tray on the sideboard in their conference room. God bless Kaitlin. Not only did she keep the business running smoothly, but she saw to all the little things that made Uniquely Yours a pleasant place to work. Jess looked forward to their weekly Friday morning meetings. Her partners' energy and enthusiasm served as a rejuvenating elixir. Each woman had her own area of expertise, and good week or bad, they propped each other up.

Pausing, she glanced around the room. Most construction offices were stark and cold or cluttered and disorganized. Not so their offices. They may currently have a boring exterior but on the inside, it was all heart. Victoria Kwan, in charge of interior design, and Kaitlin had seen to that.

The daunting duo had shooed the other three partners out and taken over. They painted the walls something called Spring Botanical Green because according to Victoria, '*not only is it soothing and relaxing, but it evokes harmony, balance, and restoration.*' Jess didn't go in for all that feng shui stuff, but she liked the effect. They'd filled the walls with impressionist prints and old architectural renderings for color and interest. Serenity Gagliardi, the firm's landscape architect, had found some decorative grow lights and added houseplants to the mix. Farmhouse-style, oak furniture rounded out the décor and made their clients—guests, Kaitlin reminded them—feel right at home.

Moving to the conference table, Jess noticed a new wreath on the wall. Kaitlin's doing, no doubt. She switched decorations throughout the building on a regular basis. This one featured artificial apples attached to grapevines. Probably a nod to the local apple and grape harvest currently in full swing. A hint of envy pricked at the base of Jess' skull. Any semblance of a homemaking gene had sadly passed her by.

Pulling out one of the ladder-back chairs, Jess took her seat at the head of the large, oval table and nodded toward the flower arrangement at its center. "The flowers are a nice touch."

"Serenity brought them in, and I just stuck them in a vase," Kaitlin said. "I love the salmon-colored roses mixed with the white snapdragons. Helps keep summer around a little while longer."

Jess rolled her eyes. "Kaitlin, you never just *stick* anything. I'll bet you spent the better part of an hour fussing over it, adding the perfect touches."

Serenity, with her Mona Lisa smile, nodded agreement.

Biting into her muffin, Jess sighed in approval. "You've done something different with these." Jess took another bite. "I like it. I wish I had half your talent in the kitchen."

"Your talents lie elsewhere, my dear." Victoria grinned and batted her eyes.

Jess hunched her shoulders and narrowed her eyes at Victoria... waiting for it.

14

"And the takeout restaurants and frozen food aisle at the grocery store are grateful," Victoria finished with a devilish twinkle in her eyes.

"Don't listen to her," Kaitlin said. "Nothing wrong with takeout or frozen food. There are so many healthy choices now." She slid a paper napkin toward Jess. "I added lemon extract and zest to the muffin batter. I think the tart adds an interesting contrast."

"You did good. I like it. As soon as Ivy shows up, we'll get started," Jess said.

"It's not like her to be late. I hope she's alright." Kaitlin rubbed her finger over a nonexistent smudge on the table as she took her seat.

"She's fine." The air held its breath as Ivy Bardot, the firm's real estate broker, breezed into the room. "Sorry all. My mom called. Dad's hip is bothering him, and she finally cajoled him into visiting the doctor. He has an appointment this afternoon, and she wanted me to know."

"Do you think it's anything serious?" Kaitlin asked.

"All those years walking neighborhoods delivering mail has probably taken a toll. I won't be surprised if he needs a hip replacement." Ivy eased off her suit jacket, draped it over the back of the chair, and sat down with the grace of a prima ballerina.

"How do you do that?" Jess asked, wishing that in Ivy's presence she didn't feel like an ox next to a gazelle.

"Do what?"

"Sit so gracefully. No chair scraping. No files thumping. No purse dropped like a sack of flour." Jess opened her clipboard and as though making her point, its metal cover clattered against the table. She sighed. "Don't mind me. I haven't reached my caffeine quota this morning."

15

"All it takes is years on the beauty pageant circuit." Soto voce Ivy mimicked her pageant handler. "Glide. Head up. Practice, practice, practice. Sit like there's a pincushion on your chair." Her chuckle rang like a small silver bell. "Personally, I'm happy those days are behind me." Maintaining her perfect posture, she reached into her satchel and withdrew several file folders.

Jess grinned trying to imagine herself in that world. Bull in a china shop came to mind. "I take it back. Dainty and refined just isn't in my wheelhouse." She glanced around the table. "Ready to get started?"

She loved this part where they all shared what they were working on. Jess went first and rattled off the construction status of their current projects and felt the familiar burst of pride. These were her babies.

Victoria went next and shared that she had an interior design inquiry from the new owner of a Victorian mansion that might lead to a complete remodel and landscaping project. She'd keep everyone posted.

Serenity reminded the group that she needed to finish the landscaping on Jess's Jackson Street flip within the next two months if she wanted to beat the rainy season. Kaitlin chimed in that she would coordinate to make sure permits are pulled and sub-contractors scheduled for any exterior cement work so Serenity wouldn't be delayed.

Ivy passed out some new listings to consider and apprised everyone on the escrow status of their current inventory. Kaitlin wrapped up the meeting by sharing the updated financials.

"Sounds like we're in good shape." Jess turned to Ivy. "You look like you're ready to burst. What haven't you told us yet?"

"The good news... a piece of land that meets all the criteria for our new offices is coming on the market. After a year of looking for just the right spot, it may finally be within our grasp. I think the owner will look at an early offer." Ivy passed around the specs for the listing.

Ivy set her clasped hands on the table and leaned forward. "The bad news... the property is owned by TLM Investments. Can't say I like their reputation."

Serenity pressed her hands together showing more excitement than Jess had seen in a while. "This looks great. Several acres. Mixed-use neighborhood with some businesses and some residential. Best of all, with this much land, Victoria and I could design the kind of storage space we need. Maybe we could add a greenhouse so I wouldn't have to constantly trek out to my parent's vineyard." Her face opened into a huge, expectant grin.

"Let's not get ahead of ourselves. I think it would have to be Ag-zoned to add a greenhouse," Jess cautioned. "Like Ivy, I'm not crazy about doing business with TLM, but I agree it's worth exploring." A knot tightened in her belly. She had good reason to avoid doing business with them. From conversations she'd overhead as a kid, she was pretty sure Thomas Miller had caused her dad's business problems. She glanced at the specs. Damn, this was exactly what they'd been looking for. Personal animosity had no place in the decision-making process.

"If we can agree on a price, I'll have our attorney produce a purchase contract that's tighter than a pickle jar lid," Ivy said. "No wiggle room for this guy."

"Keep us posted. Is there anything else to discuss?" She paused. No one said anything. "Then I'm heading out to our Jackson Street flip." Glancing at Victoria, she asked, "Are you still planning to stop by and take a final look, now that my crew's opened up the floorplan?"

"I'll be there in about forty-five minutes." Victoria smiled at Ivy who'd started to say something. "Don't worry. I haven't forgotten about you. I'll stage your new listing this afternoon."

"Perfect. I've already prepped the owners, and they're excited to see what you have in mind," Ivy said. "Oh, and Serenity, they love what you did with their yard. They're kicking themselves they didn't do something like it sooner while they could have enjoyed it." She winked. "I'll bet once they're settled in their new home, you'll be one of their first calls."

Jess stood. "Great work everyone."

VICTORIA STOOD IN THE middle of the great room of the Jackson Street flip, squinting—her arms outstretched, palms flat, and thumbs pointing toward each other. Slowly she swiveled her torso framing each section between her hands. Jess stood in the doorway and bit back a grin. The crew looked bemused, not sure what to make of the tiny Asian woman exclaiming over nothing but walls reduced to studs.

"Does it pass muster?" Jess grimaced. "Please tell me I don't need to move anything."

Victoria bent and picked up the blueprints at her feet and unrolled them. She studied the area one last time. "Nope, everything is exactly to spec. This house will make someone a fantastic home." She walked into what would be the kitchen. "I'm glad you decided to go with the garden window. It will be nice to stand at the sink and look into the yard."

"If you recall, I was outvoted by the rest of you, but I'm glad I was," Jess said. "It cost a little more, but it's a nice feature." And she could just see the wife at the sink doing dishes and her husband sneaking up behind her, putting his arms around her, and nibbling on her neck. The picture made her heart beat faster.

Victoria lowered her voice. "Speaking of nice features... who's the new guy? You know I love broody James Dean types."

Jess knew exactly who her friend meant. "That's our new hire, Devin." She pointed her finger at Victoria. "Don't get any ideas. He's a good worker, and I don't want to lose him."

Victoria scowled and put her hands on her hips. "That guy you had to fire came on to *me*. Not my fault he wouldn't take no for an answer. I didn't encourage him, and I was simply on site to do my job."

Pushing her fingertips into her temple, Jess drew a deep breath. "True. The guy was a jerk and would have been fired sooner or later."

"Besides, I can't help it if men buzz around me like bees in a field of clover."

Jess' lips curved in a mischievous grin. "Doesn't hurt that every time you bring home a tatted construction worker your mother is not pleased." Victoria chuckled. Just the response Jess had hoped for. Tension eased.

"An added benefit. Haven't met a stuffy construction worker yet. Can't say the same for the men my mom wants to set me up with. Boring." Victoria drew out the word and rolled her eyes. Glancing over her shoulder, a sultry smile crept across her face. The men, who had been staring, quickly ducked their heads and got back to work. Victoria laughed at their reaction. "Seriously though, you need to stop treating dating like it's a boxing match. Lower your guard. Enjoy yourself."

Jess felt that funny thump in her chest. It was smart to keep men at a safe distance until she got to know them well. She couldn't help it if work kept her too busy to bother with dating. "Any other questions about the project?"

"No questions." Victoria rolled up her blueprints and collected her purse. "I've picked out the paint colors and marked on the plans where to use them. Kaitlin said the cabinets, wood flooring, and tile for the kitchen and bathrooms will arrive at the end of next week. I'll order the countertops, carpet, and light fixtures soon so they'll be ready when you need them."

Jess crossed her fingers. "So far no major hitches on any of the projects. Rollo's will go on the market in about three weeks. His crew will get a week off and then start on the one closing escrow shortly." Her gaze swept the room and she let the wonder of it all seep into her.

"It's pretty amazing, alright." Victoria faced Jess and quirked a brow. "It's Friday. Any big plans for the weekend?"

"The usual. Drinks with the crew when we knock off. Tomorrow I'll keep making inroads on my house remodel." Jess sighed. "Sunday dinner with my folks."

"Girlfriend, you need to get a life." Victoria shook her finger at Jess. "There's still time to join the rest of us for our weekend getaway to the city."

Jess stifled the groan building in her throat and forced herself to relax. "I'm sure you guys will have a good time, but body wraps and facials followed by a night of crowded dance floors in a too tight dress—not my idea of a good time."

"She who refuses to dip her toe in the water will shrivel up like an old prune." Victoria angled her head toward Devin. "That new guy has been sneaking peeks at you. A little flirting might do you a world of good."

"First" —Jess held up one finger— "who says he's not looking at you?" She held up a second finger. "Second, dating guys on the crew breaks one of my personal rules. It can lead to all sorts of problems. They're either too young or too married. And third," she held up a final finger in the universal signal to leave her alone. "I'm fine with my life. When Mr. Right wanders into view, then I'll start dating. Till then...?" she shrugged, "I'm in no hurry." Much better to take things slow and avoid potential landmines.

"I'd be happy to set you up with some guys I know. No sense waiting for Mr. Right to happen by. Take some initiative."

"Thanks but no thanks. The bad boys you date to annoy your mom are not my type."

"Suit yourself. I'm off to the store to buy you a bucket of moisturizing cream." She wiggled her fingers over her shoulder as she walked away. "Pruney."

# Chapter Three

*HER SOCIAL LIFE WAS not a shriveled prune.* She knew how to have fun. Wasn't she here at happy hour to do just that? Jess snagged her beer off the bar and strode through the darkened room. The place wasn't much aesthetically but it had plenty of on-tap beer, great bar food, and banks of televisions lining the walls, showcasing every sports team currently playing.

Rising to her tiptoes, Jess slid on to one of the tall, wooden stools and studied her crew gathered around the table. In addition to Devin, there was Jeremy, the youngest, Bryan the oldest and only married one, Penny, the only female, and Jamal.

"That was some game last night," Jeremy said with the enthusiasm of youth.

Jess chimed in. "Felt like throwing something at the television, though. Refs couldn't keep those penalty flags in their pockets."

"Hey, it's the Raiders. What do you expect? Someone looks cross-eyed, and out come the flags." Bryan rolled his eyes.

"Personally, I'm counting down the days until basketball season," Penny said.

"I'm right there with ya." Jamal exchanged a high-five with Penny. "Maybe the Kings will finally pull it together this year." He leaned closer to Penny and his voice grew husky. "We'll have to go to some games together this year."

Penny lowered her lashes. "I'd like that."

Unless Jess was way off base, there was more than friendship going on here. Not that she had anything against romance, as long as any associated drama stayed off the construction site. Hard enough to keep good employees without folks taking sides in an argument. She stressed safety in the workplace but right behind that came maintaining a congenial, non-judgmental environment.

Studying Devin out of the corner of her eye, she noticed he was nursing a soda, silently watching the banter among his new co-workers. The soda didn't fit the bad boy image of him she'd formed in her mind, but the aloofness did. Jess hoped he'd open up and begin forming a bond with the others. Might as well see if she could nudge him along.

"So Devin, are you rooting for any of the Northern California teams?" Jess asked as the waitress placed the appetizers Jess had ordered on the table. As expected, the guys pounced on the chicken wings and onion rings.

"Not really." His laser-like blue eyes bored in to her until she wanted to squirm. His mouth quirked up at one corner and Jess felt like she was the butt end of some private joke. "Haven't formed any attachments yet." He ran his hand up and down the side of the glass. The condensation pooled on the table. "My dad favored the Niners. They were winners. In my rebellious youth, if my dad was for it, I was against it." Bringing the glass to his lips, he took a sip.

"Happens in lots of families. Can't wait for my kids to reach their teenage years." Bryan rolled his eyes and broke apart an onion ring. The aroma of fried onion rose on the steam. "Didn't you say you moved here from New Jersey?"

Devin nodded, his face wary.

"Then we'll try not to hold it against you if you're a fan of one of those East Coast teams." Bryan clinked his glass against Devin's.

A grin—not a polite 'I know I have to interact with you' grin—but a real grin that brought out his dimples. His face lost that haunted look, at least momentarily. "Been rooting for the Ravens. They've got that scrappy underdog thing going."

"Then you should consider switching allegiances. The Raiders seem to have a lock on the underdog title lately," Bryan said.

"Noted." Devin eased back on his stool and out of the conversation.

"Besides watching football, what's everyone doing this weekend?" Jess asked.

"Jamal and I are going apple picking tomorrow. Then dinner and a movie," Penny volunteered.

"And I'm looking forward to that promised apple pie on Sunday." Jamal winked at Penny who blushed.

"Promised the wife and kids a trip to Yosemite. Got reservations at that fancy lodge, so making a weekend of it," offered Bryan.

"Visiting a friend in San Francisco," Devin said.

Did everyone have something to look forward to but her? Jess chewed on her lip. Victoria may have a point. She needed a life.

"What about you?" asked Penny. "Working on your house again, and Sunday dinner with your folks?"

Was she that predictable? "Actually, I'm heading off for a spa weekend with my girlfriends." Jess crossed her fingers behind her back. At least she hoped she could still take her friends up on their offer. She'd text Ivy as soon as she left the bar.

"Really?" Penny's surprised expression said it all. "You and pampering? It's going to take me a minute to wrap my mind around that image."

"I have my girly side." Jess hoped her smile transmitted light and frivolous. "Nothing like a good exfoliation to make a woman feel pretty." Maybe she did need to shake up her routine a little. Just because her college boyfriend had stabbed her in the back, and the dickhead she'd dated after college had tried to steal her clients didn't mean she couldn't trust all men.

"On that note, I'm outta here." Bryan drained the last of his beer. "If I don't get home and help my wife pack, she'll have my hide."

"Me too," said Jamal. "Promised my mom I'd stop by and fix her garbage disposal."

"And I'm off to meet my sister at the mall," said Penny.

Chairs scraped as everyone except Devin and Jess pushed away from the table. She wiped her damp palms on her jeans and wracked her brain for a topic of conversation. Hopefully one with a graceful exit line. The powerful attraction she felt for Devin was unnerving.

"Is this a childhood friend you'll be visiting this weekend?" Jess felt satisfied she'd come up with a nice, neutral question. One that would get him to talk about himself.

"Yeah, he is. How'd you figure that?" Devin leaned back and hooked his arm over the back of the chair. He reminded her of one of those malt shop bad boys who didn't need to work at being cool. His pose pulled his t-shirt snuggly across his broad chest showing off hard-earned contours and ridges.

"It seemed like a reasonable assumption. You haven't been back in the area long. It's unlikely you'd spend the weekend in the city with a new friend, so it had to be someone you knew from before."

Again those crystalline blue eyes bored into her. "I've known Law all my life. When I left, we stayed in touch."

"Law, that's an unusual name."

"His given name is Lawrence but other than his parents, people use it on pain of death." His dimples reappeared. "He won't admit it, but when we were little, he had a thing for my sister."

"Usually when a friend is interested in a guy's sister that causes friction between them. You seem okay with it."

"I am. Law's a good guy and would be good for my by-the-book sister. They haven't seen each other in years." He lifted one shoulder and drew a swirl with his finger in the moisture pooled on the table from his glass. "If it had been serious, they'd have found a way to see each other. Sounds like you're familiar with the protective older brother syndrome."

A lump formed in her throat, and she shook her head. "Much to my dad's disappointment, no boys. One younger sister who just got married. Another reason my dad is on my back to quit construction. My sister's settled down. It's time I did the same." Her foot started bouncing under the table. What possessed her to tell him about that?

Without taking a breath, she hurried on before he had a chance to delve into her personal life. He wasn't the only one who could be tight-lipped. "Serenity, you met her on the job site, has three brothers, who give anyone she's even looked at a hard time. Large Italian family, so I've seen the process in action."

"She's the one in charge of the landscaping projects?"

"That's the one."

Devin's forehead wrinkled in confusion. "Your dad wants you to quit the construction business? Why? You seem to be doing alright."

Damn. He wasn't going to let it go. "My dad's old-fashioned and thinks construction is too tough for women." She blew out a breath. "I know he's disappointed in my career choice, but I'm learning to live with it because I love what I do."

"We should start a support group, 'Uniting Against Parental Expectations Anonymous.'." The corners of his mouth ticked up. "Probably wouldn't even have to provide donuts to get people to join."

His dry humor was infectious. Her breath came easier and the air seemed lighter. "I think we'd need a big serving of Mac and Cheese plus a rousing chorus of Kum Ba Yah to set the tone." She grinned back at him proud of her attempt at banter.

"Why Miss Winters, are you teasing me?"

His chuckle sounded like it hadn't been used in a while. A bit hesitant but ready to blow off the dust.

"I guess I am." She steepled her fingers in front of her mouth. Not sure she should ask the question on her mind but decided to forge ahead anyway. "If you don't mind my asking, what qualifies you to join our bad parent support group?"

His eyelids slipped to half-mast. "My dad wanted someone like him... tough, ruthless, willing to do whatever it took to come out on top. He never cared who he trampled." Devin shook his glass and the ice rattled. A muscle ticked along his jaw. "I couldn't be that person."

She covered his hand with hers understanding why he was hesitant to talk about his family. Still, she wished he was less cagey about his past. "Then we're both better off following our own paths, no matter how painful."

His eyes met hers, and her breath caught. She could get lost in those eyes. Her fingers tingled where they made contact with his skin. She cleared her throat. "It's time for me to hit the road." She scooted her empty beer mug away. "I'll see you on Monday. Have a good time this weekend."

"You too," he said.

His voice hit her like sangria. Rich, and fruity, but with a heat as it traveled down her throat and a kick as it landed in her stomach. Men with secrets weren't to be trusted. No matter the pull she felt for him, she'd proceed with caution.

# Chapter Four

DEVIN HAD SPENT THE day helping Law inventory the supplies at his night club. Now they sat at the bar, relaxing, and trying to decide which of the many lovely ladies might keep them company for the evening. His head swung toward the front of the night club as though attached to a lead line. Gazing across the crowd, he could see he wasn't the only one. Every eye in the place was riveted on the five women poised at the entrance to the room, laughing and giving the impression they were oblivious to the attention directed their way.

The Maître D' hustled over, so eager to greet the new guests, he almost tripped. He stopped short of bowing and scraping when he reached them, but just barely.

God... they were all gorgeous, but Jess in that silky sapphire blue sheath and take-no-prisoners silver stilettos stopped his heart. The *whomp, whomp* of the dance music and the hundreds of conversations faded into white noise. He couldn't tear his gaze away and feared he'd be caught gawking like an awe-struck schoolboy. A quick sweep of the room told him he was in good company.

"Who knew such perfection existed, let alone would walk into my club." Law's voice was pitched a notch higher than his usual baritone.

He must have noticed because he cleared his throat. "I'm thinking a round of drinks for the lovely ladies is in order so I can introduce myself."

"The drink idea is fine," Devin said. "But I can introduce you."

"Are you shitting me? You know them?"

"Two of them anyway. That stunning little blonde in the blue dress is my boss." Devin took a sip of his club soda to wet his dry mouth. A fortifying breath helped steady his rapidly-beating heart.

"That's the construction lady?" Law's eyebrows shot to his hairline. "No wonder I can't tempt you away from that job." Law straightened his expensive silk tie. "What are we waiting for? Introduce us already. We can pick up the conversation later about your dad."

Devin glanced around the room and agreed with Law. Better stake out their claim before the other single males beat them to it. A few had already pushed away from the bar. Wiping his sweaty palms down his slacks, he and Law headed for the booth where Jess and her friends sat. Devin stopped his friend when they'd taken a few steps. "She doesn't know who my dad is. You'll keep quiet about that?"

"Of course. Tonight I'm your wingman," Law said.

Jess glanced up as they stopped at their table. Well, they all glanced up, but hers were the only set of eyes that mattered to Devin. Surprise first filled those cornflower blue eyes but was swiftly replaced by pleasure. At least he hoped it was pleasure.

"Didn't expect to run into you this weekend," Devin said. "What are the chances in a city the size of San Francisco that we'd end up at the same club?"

"If you'd asked me an hour ago, I would have said, zero. Obviously, I'd have been wrong. Let me introduce you to my friends." Jess pointed to each woman as she said their names. "And you know Kaitlin. I'd invite you to join us," her gaze swept the booth, "but as you can see, there's no room."

Law raised his arm and crooked his finger. A server immediately appeared at his side. "Would you prepare my private room, please? We'll be over in a minute." The server pivoted and hurried toward the back of the room to the left of the DJ station.

Devin smothered a smile at the incredulous expressions on the women's faces. "Allow me to introduce my friend. Ladies this is Law Newhouse. He owns this place." Extending his hand to Jess who was sitting on the outside edge, he helped her rise. Even in those death-defying heels, the top of her head barely grazed his cheek. Law offered his hand to Ivy who was sitting on the other outside edge. When she stood beside him, he tucked her hand into the crook of his arm. Kaitlin, Victoria, and Serenity accepted the men's help as each scooted to the edge of the booth. Once everyone was ready, they made their way around the dance floor to Law's private room. Devin felt the dagger-like stares of the other men as these delectable creatures were shuttled from their grasps. He didn't care. Tough luck to them.

Jess' perfume teased his senses. It was something exotic with a hint of spice. Not her usual hint of roses. When he touched the bare skin of her back above the scoop of her dress as he ushered her into the space, his fingers tingled. Her slight shiver in response had heat pooling in his groin.

He followed her gaze and watched her brows rise as she assessed the area. The side of the room facing the dance floor was all glass. The sliding doors were pulled shut after they entered which made conversation easier and the space more intimate. Short sections of plush banquet seating lined the other three walls. Small drink tables separated each section. Original modern artwork adorned the space above the seating. The walls were painted a deep red. Pinpoint lighting in the ceiling spotlighted the paintings making the room dim but not dark. Small glass tables dotted the open space and held battery-powered candles that added a romantic touch.

"*Now this is how I like to roll,*" murmured Ivy in that sultry voice of hers. She smiled at Law, her big, brown eyes shining. "R.E.S.P.E.C.T. Thank you, Law."

"My pleasure."

Devin guffawed at his friend's preening under the elegant, black woman's approval.

Law turned to the waiting servers. "Get them whatever they want to drink, and bring my usual appetizer order." One server departed and the other stationed herself at the side of the room. "Ladies, feel free to mingle on the dance floor and if you find someone you'd like to spend the evening with, please invite them to join us." He raised Ivy's hand to his lips. "I hope you'll do me the honor of being my partner while you're here. Would you like to dance?"

"I thought you'd never ask," Ivy said.

Devin hung back, and so did Jess, as everyone else filtered out.

"Your friendship with Law explains a lot," Jess said.

"How so?" Devin motioned toward the seating and sat when she did.

"You gave the impression that you're low on funds." She cocked her head, studied his face. "I know my pocketbook gulped when I learned how much it cost. Without some serious green and reservations made months in advance, you don't get in. That's why I was surprised to see you here."

A flash or irritation tightened his jaw. He knew his past didn't exactly make him a prize. "It's good to have friends." He arched one brow and let the tingling in his chest take over. "Surprised to see me, but pleased, I hope?" She thought for a minute and he held his breath. Spending time with her outside of work probably wasn't a good idea. He was too attracted to her and once she found out he was Thomas Miller's son, she might not want to have anything to do with him.

"Yes, I was." She held up one finger to ward him off as he started to shift closer. "But I'm not sure it's a good idea for me to get to cozy with an employee. Too much at stake and too much potential for trouble. Friendship is all I have to offer." She drummed her fingers against her thighs and sighed. "But we're here tonight, so I suppose it wouldn't hurt to get to know each other better."

He released a shaky breath. This was good and bad. Good she wanted to get to know him. Bad she wanted to get to know him. Until he had more information about all the people who'd been his father's victims, he couldn't let anyone know his connection to TLM Investments. He needed people to talk to him, not shun him. "There's not much to tell. But friends works, and if we discover we have a lot in common…"

"Just so you know, on Monday I'll be transferring you to Bill's blue team." She shifted away putting a little space between them and he missed her thigh pressed to his. "It has nothing to do with you. I need an extra finish carpenter for a few weeks so I'm doing some shuffling."

"I'd heard." One corner of his mouth ticked up at her expression. "Someone on Bill's crew talked to someone on our crew." He shrugged. "Word spreads faster than a cheetah in full stride. I doubt much stays secret." Folding his hands in his lap, he asked, "Now about us getting to know each other better, if we went out together... as friends... what would we do? Dinner? Movies? Sporting events? What do you do in your free time?" A big part of him wanted to learn everything he could about her and it had nothing to do with uncovering information about his dad.

"I spend a lot of time renovating my house. I like to hike. Go wine tasting. Dinner and a movie would be fine. I like doing outdoors stuff." She shrugged again. "Basically I'm a pretty simple person."

She swiveled to face him and their knees bumped. A jolt of pleasure raced up his spine, and the roaring in his ears almost drowned out her next words.

"If you're looking for someone to provide home-cooked meals, I'm not your girl."

"Then I suppose it's a good thing that I can cook." He lightly ran his finger over the back of her hand and marveled at the softness. "You don't strike me as a simple person." He studied her taking in the color rising in her cheeks and the way her eyes lowered. "What do you say if I stop by next weekend and help you with one of your house projects? As a friend. It would give me a chance to pick up some pointers for work, and I could make us dinner."

He watched the shy smile steal across her face. It was so different than her usual take-charge attitude.

"That would be nice."

His heart constricted at the wonder in her voice. Didn't she expect men to do nice things for her? His heart thudded in his chest. And here he planned to pump her for information. She probably knew something about what caused her dad's business problems and maybe knew about others in the trade his dad had swindled. She'd been in the business for a long time. She must have heard rumors. He needed a place to start digging but he still felt like a heel.

She cleared her throat. "In your free time, what do you like to do?"

"I hate being cooped up, so like you, I prefer being outside." It felt strange opening up to someone—even in a minimal way—like a musty room that needed airing. "I inherited a small pontoon boat when my grandpa passed two years ago." Guilt pierced his soul. He hadn't been in any shape to attend his funeral and regretted missing the chance to say goodbye. "Now that I'm back in the area, I can finally use it. I'm not fond of fishing but I like floating around on the open water. Putting in to shore when a spot catches my fancy."

"That's another thing that would be fun to do together, especially while the weather is still nice." She bit her lip. "You said you were born here. Are your parents still in the area?"

Icy fingers pressed into his lower back. "Yes, but we're estranged." He glanced up as a server wheeled in a portable food bar. The aroma of nachos, bacon, and French fries hovered in the air. Another server carried in the drink orders and set them on a table. Relief flooded his body. "Should we get some food, or would you like to hit the dance floor first?"

She looked at him, curiosity in her eyes but said, "Food first, dancing later."

"As I suspected."

Laughing, Jess said, "I guess you do know me."

"Why do you think I offered to make you dinner?" He extended his hand and pleasure bloomed in the center of his chest when she slipped her hand into his. There was something very right about walking beside her, their arms brushing. Picking up a plate, he passed it to her. She said friendship only but he wasn't sure he believed her.

Jess separated a section of nachos and placed it on her plate. Bacon-wrapped prawns came next. "Oh look, mini sliders and chili cheese fries." She sucked in an excited breath. "Specialty olives. I love the ones stuffed with garlic." She added a few of those to her plate. "I'm glad to see Law included some healthier choices in the mix. My friends will appreciate that."

He savored the flirty look she gave him. "Law learned early to trust the advice of his female staff when making menu selections." Devin loaded up his plate as the sight and smell of the food increased his hunger pangs.

Strolling back to their seats, Jess popped an olive into her mouth. She closed her eyes and moaned. The tip of her tongue circled her lips to capture the brine from the olive. Devin swallowed hard. A powerful urge to wrap his lips around that tempting pink bud engulfed him.

"You do know that friends share stuff. Talking about your problems with your parents might help," Jess said.

He bobbled the plate he carried, and the romantic thoughts he'd harbored hit the floor. As soon as they sat, the server delivered their drinks. He took a sip of his club soda while he organized his thoughts searching for a way to reveal something without offering clues to his identity. "I have a brother in the area, and I want to patch things up with him first. If that goes well, then I'll see."

Jess laid a hand on his arm. "Growing up, I saw all these happy families on television. My friend's families seemed happy. Idyllic. I wanted that for myself. Reality doesn't always align itself to the way we expect the world to be."

She dropped her hand and he missed the comforting weight of it. "No it doesn't. Best to set dreams aside. That way you've got a chance to duck the punch when it comes." Devin pressed his lips together waiting for the pain to pass.

"I don't buy it. Uniquely Yours was a dream once, and would have stayed that way if we hadn't taken steps to make it happen. Never give up on your dreams. Surely you believe that."

"Some part of me must." He swallowed and shifted mental gears. "Tell me about this house you're remodeling. Is it a complete gut job or just some spit and polish?" Even to his own ears his voice sounded like he smoked a pack of cigarettes a day.

"Closer to a gut job. Since I was a kid, Victorian architecture fascinated me. In my mind those houses represented happy families and a gentler way of life."

He nudged her shoulder with his. "You sound like a romantic. Bet you had the same doll house my sister did."

Her eyes danced with amusement. "Doubt it. I built my own." She shrugged, obviously pleased with herself. "Last year, a wreck of a place came on the market. The old lady needed a bit of modernizing, but her bones were good so I scooped it up. Victoria worked with me on a remodel plan. I've been taking it a room at a time. My current project is the upstairs guest bathroom." She glanced at him and grinned. "Sorry, but the kitchen is low on my list, so you'll be working with appliances from the seventies."

"I can work with that. If the oven heats and burners on the stove are operational, I'm good to go." He sat back and chuckled. "For a minute there, I was afraid I would have to figure out how to work a wood burning stove."

He pulled out his phone. "Since I won't see you much this week, let me get your number so we can coordinate next weekend. I appreciate the chance to improve my skills."

The sliding door opened as he tucked the phone back into his pocket. Laughter poured into the room along with all the bodies. Their alone time was over... for now. Devin couldn't check the disappointment that pressed on his chest but looked forward to next weekend. For the present, he'd put on his social face and pretend he didn't wish all the others would disappear into the air like smoke. "You ready to hit the dance floor?"

# Chapter Five

TRUDGING UP THE WALK to her parent's modest ranch-style home, Jess pinched the bridge of her nose, wishing the mild hangover had responded to the aspirin she'd taken. Note to self—no heavy partying on Saturday night. Facing her dad and making nice during their weekly Sunday dinner was hard enough when her head was clear and her stomach wasn't queasy.

Jess knocked and then opened the door. "Hello, I'm here," she called into the darkened entry. Since her parents spent the bulk of their time in the back of the house, they seldom bothered to pull the drapes in the living room. Shadows and silence greeted her—the story of her life. She got along with her mom but in the continual tug of war between father and daughter, her mom pulled on her dad's end of the rope.

Following the sound of the television and the smell of over-cooked pot roast, Jess made her way to the family room. Pausing behind her dad's recliner, she bent and kissed the top of his balding head. "Hi pops. How are you? How's the game?"

"Fucking refs don't know shit. Penalties every other play." Her dad, Gerry, had been in a foul mood since the start of football season when his beloved Raiders hadn't lived up to expectations.

Jess tasted the familiar bitterness on her tongue. Not a 'hi, how are you' or a 'glad to see you' in return. Not even a pat on the hand. No sign of affection. Her sister, Hannah, rose from the sofa where she sat next to her husband, Bob. She rolled her eyes in commiseration, and the two women hugged.

Silently Hannah mouthed, "I want to hear about your weekend."

Jess mouthed back, "Later," and grinned at her sister who gave her a thumbs up.

Next stop, the kitchen, where her mom stirred lumpy gravy. Jess kissed her mom, Darlene, on the cheek and draped an arm across her shoulders. "Smells good," Jess lied. Cooking had never been her mom's forte. She'd been much happier handling the books and such for her dad's construction business. Jess might have been forced to learn to cook in self-defense but Hannah had picked up that mantle. "You should let Hannah and I host Sunday dinners sometimes so all the work doesn't fall on you."

Her father bellowed from his recliner, "What? In that dump you call a home, or that tiny apartment of Hannah's?" She heard the *thunk* as Gerry righted his chair ready for battle. "Not good enough for you here?"

Jess' stomach churned with frustration and acid. He knew how to push her buttons. It stung that he didn't respect her decisions. Her house was a good investment. "No Dad, we love having dinner here. Right Hannah?"

"Definitely." But Jess saw Hannah crinkle her nose at their dad.

"I'm just trying to make it a little easier on Mom. She gets stuck with the cooking every week. Thought it might be nice to spread the work around. Let Mom relax once in a while."

"Yeah and what would you serve? Take out?" Her father's chuckle was about as friendly as a rattlesnake. Jess kept hoping he'd eventually revert to his old self—the one who had let her follow him around and taught her to love the construction trade. He'd cared once. Her hope was that he could again.

"Got me there, Dad." Though bile burned in her throat she decided it was time to divert his attention from her shortcomings. "I like the new built-in bookcase and cabinet you added to the living room. Looks nice."

Her father grunted and returned his focus to the game. Daughter dismissed.

Jess sighed as Hannah joined them in the kitchen and gave Jess a one-armed hug. "Can we set the table for you, Mom?" Jess asked.

"That would be nice dears." Darlene patted her eldest daughter's hand. "Don't mind him Jess. You know that's just the way he is. He doesn't mean anything by it."

As she and Hannah set to work pulling plates, glasses, and silverware from the cupboards and drawers, Jess wished what her mother said was true. But in her heart-of-hearts—the one that concealed the deepest hurts and the greatest joys—she knew her father was an unhappy man. He'd never gotten the son he'd wanted to follow in his footsteps. His business had tanked and never fully recovered after some bad business deal he refused to talk about. His reputation had also taken a nose dive—a sore spot to this day. He'd had to sell their big, beautiful home in an upscale neighborhood and downsize to this as he struggled to stay afloat. Everyone and everything in his life had disappointed him.

Once they'd taken their places, Jess surveyed the scene. Here they all were, gathered at the table for Sunday dinner. To the casual observer, the tableau must look ideal. Mom, dad, and offspring breaking bread together. Were all families like hers? Dysfunctional, once you scrapped below the surface layer?

"Hannah told me you might be looking at a piece of property where you can build your new offices," Bob said as he passed the bowl of soggy green beans to his wife.

"Ivy found the perfect lot in a mixed-use neighborhood. We didn't want to be stuck in a completely commercial area and lots like these are hard to come by. It's just under two acres which gives us the option of building something big enough to include rental space." Jess accepted the bowl of green beans from her mom and spooned some on to her plate.

"Sounds perfect. I know developing your own office space has been a dream of yours for a while," Bob said.

"Yup, you need a fancy schmancy building to go with that fancy schmancy Construction Management degree." Gerry made air quotes with his fingers. "He stabbed a chunk of beef with his fork and shoved it in his mouth. He kept talking while he chewed. "In my day, we learned on the job and worked out of a trailer."

Jess' fingernails bit into her palm. She used the pain to keep the words she wanted to say from tumbling out. What was the point? Her father wasn't going to change. The best she could hope for was to keep the peace. "And you did good, Dad, but times have changed and clients expect something a little flashier."

"I'll give you that. Gotta keep up with the competition. Just hate to see you spend so much money. Never know when the economy will tank." He tore a roll in half with a vengeance.

"No one can plan for every contingency but the firm has been saving for years and we've built up a nice cushion." She readjusted the napkin on her lap. "Besides, we might not get it. TLM Investments owns it and they're not the most reputable firm to do business with."

Her dad's fork clattered against his plate, and he stood so quickly his chair tipped over, hitting the floor with a *thud*. Without a word, he stalked out of the room.

That empty, baffled sensation burst in Jess' brain. "What did I do now?" She must have interpreted those whispered conversations she'd overhead as a child correctly. TLM Investment had played a role in her dad's downfall.

"Nothing dear. Your father and Thomas Miller go way back, and there's a lot of bad blood between them." She smiled and slathered some butter on her roll. "Now everyone eat up and let's enjoy our meal."

---

DEVIN SAT ON A park bench, one leg crossed over the other, waiting for his brother. Phil had agreed to meet him, share a cup of coffee, and Devin hoped, make progress toward rebuilding their childhood bond. Eight years Phil's senior, Devin had been the big brother the boy had desperately wanted to look up to. He was also the big brother least likely to be the moral compass Phil had needed. Devin had acted out, rebelled against the example their father set. Driven by resentment. Fueled by shame.

Maybe that had been the best way to address his moral outrage. Maybe not. At fourteen, hormones running rampant, Devin had discovered his father's unscrupulous dealings. He'd lashed out, wanting to hurt his father for not staying on the pedestal he'd put him on. Skipping school. Minor shoplifting that his dad had made go away. Fallen in with the party crowd. No wonder Law's parents had tried to keep them apart. Luckily they'd relented after Devin was sent away to military school. Now in his mid-thirties, Devin was finally finding his way. Straightening his back and tilting his head to gaze at the sky, Devin filled his lungs and slowly let the breath out. Old resentments died hard.

Spying his brother hurrying toward him, phone to his ear, Devin stood. Phil stopped when he reached him, disconnected his call, and slipped his phone in his pocket. Devin could tell his brother didn't know what to do. Awkwardness hung in the air. Phil's hands were on the brink of reaching out but hesitant. He appeared to be trying to decide if they should go in his pockets, hang at his sides, or if he should shake hands. His feet shuffled. Devin took the initiative and wrapped his brother in a quick, loose hug, slapping him on the back. The wall between them opened and cracks appeared in the initial tension.

"You're looking good," Devin said. And Phil did. With a sport-coat over a t-shirt, jeans, and pricey Italian loafers, his brother radiated power and wealth. His blonde hair was styled in a fashionably mussed way and trendy stubble outlined his jaw. Phil had their father's fair coloring while Devin had inherited their mother's darkness.

"Thanks," Phil said. "You're looking," —the pause was telling— "healthy."

"I am. It's been a long haul to get here, but I feel like I've gotten my life back on track." By an unspoken agreement, they started walking down the busy downtown street. The traffic noise and folks out to see the sights on a pleasant Sunday afternoon, provided the privacy Devin sought for a sensitive conversation.

"And you're enjoying working in the construction industry?" Phil asked.

"If by construction industry, you mean general laborer, then yes. I like working with my hands."

"How's Madison? I haven't heard from her in a while. Any chance she might come out for a visit now that you're here?"

"Madison's fine. She loves being a pharmacist. Living in New Jersey suits her." Devin chuckled. "Who'd have thought that our sister would turn into a Jersey girl?"

Phil laughed too. "Surely it's not come to that. Hard to imagine our quiet, serous sister being sarcastic and edgy." The levity took the sharp edge off his face, making him more approachable.

"On a more refined scale but afraid so. As far as visiting... she's thought about it. She'd like to see you again and meet your wife," Devin took a fortifying breath. It was time to address the elephant in the room—"but she doesn't want anything to do with Dad."

"She hates him that much?" The hard edge returned to Phil's face and voice.

"Hate is a strong word, but she's never going to respect him and doesn't want to associate with him as long as he thinks it's okay to cheat people."

"You still on that jag? Our father's some kind of villain, and you're hell bent on poisoning Madison with your venom?" Phil scrubbed a hand over his hair. "He is our father and gave us all a pretty nice life. Doesn't that count for something?"

Devin compressed his lips and waited for the anger percolating through his veins to pass. "Speak for yourself. My life was pretty shitty." He stared into his brother's eyes. "Not that I didn't bear some responsibility, but a lot of what happened is the direct result of the shame I felt at being his son."

"Dad wasn't exactly thrilled to claim you either."

Breathing slowly, Devin waited for his heart rate to slow so the anger he felt wouldn't come through. He wanted to sound calm and rational. "You do know that if dad's business dealings aren't illegal, they are definitely unethical."

"You're not going to let it go, are you?" Phil shrugged. "I work with Dad every day, and I've never seen anything to support your allegations. As far as I know, everything is done on the up and up." Defensiveness laced Phil's words, and his hands clenched. "Dad does his thing at the company and I do mine."

"Fair enough. Maybe Dad's changed since I was a boy." Devin doubted that, but convincing his brother otherwise would take time. Phil's livelihood depended on the success of the firm. It would be hard for him to let go of his illusions, even if he suspected something fishy was going on. "Are you going to tell dad I'm back in town?"

His brother narrowed his eyes and then his face shifted to one of resignation. "I don't think so. No sense poking the hornet's nest. I doubt he'll be pleased and I'd prefer to avoid stirring up old wounds."

Relief flowed through his veins. That's good. It wouldn't do to have their dad checking up on him. Devin had to be patient. Thomas Miller had been bilking folks in the industry for years, and no one had said anything yet. The collapse of the company wasn't imminent. He had time to bring Phil around and get him out of TLM Investments. "Tell me about your wife and this baby you're expecting." He lightly pushed Phil's arm. "My little brother is going to be a dad. I'm looking forward to meeting your wife."

# Chapter Six

EVERY TIME THEY SOLD one of their flips, the team made a concerted effort to meet at the house and hand over the keys to the new owners. The excitement and wonder as the homeowners wandered from room to room exclaiming over each new feature they discovered reminded the partners why they'd formed Uniquely Yours in the first place.

"It does my heart good to help make someone's dream come true," Kaitlin said after the happy couple had thrown their arms around a stoic Ivy and then dashed back into the house, trailed by both sets of parents. "They hated renting but didn't want to move away from family. I'm glad we could help."

"Their letter did it for me," added Serenity. "They'd fought back from job loss and financial hardship to own their own home. They didn't make excuses. They scrimped and saved and simply asked for a shot. Second chances. That's what we're in business for."

Ivy straightened the jacket of her designer suit. "Theirs wasn't the best offer, but they did make the most compelling case... and with a baby on the way, I agree, we made the right choice."

Jess felt that happy glow inside she always did when they matched the right buyer with the right property. "Ladies, I think we can chalk another one in the win column." She sighed and let the good feeling sink a little deeper. "And Serenity, creating a plot for a vegetable garden when we learned they love to garden... inspired. Come next spring I can visualize them planting some tomatoes and such, the baby in one of those little swings nearby... Perfect."

"Good deed doing is nourishment for the soul." Victoria tapped her chest several times in rapid succession and drew in a breath. "I do so love to wallow in all the joy we create."

"Much as I'd like to stay and bask in all this joy," —sarcasm coated Ivy's words— "we do need to look at a new listing and decide whether or not we want to make it our next flip." She glanced at her watch. "I'm set to show property to clients in a few hours, so if we're going to do this, we need to get moving."

"Ivy. Ivy. Ivy. Don't pretend that hard-nosed businesswoman routine with us," Victoria teased. "We all know that under that bluster lurks the spirit of a baby goat."

Ivy leveled an incredulous look at Victoria. "There are times when I question your sanity. A baby goat? Me? Honestly?"

"Yeah. Baby goat. You know they're all bouncy and spritely and cute. Joy personified," Victoria said.

Serenity rolled her eyes. "When exactly have you seen Ivy bouncy and spritely and cute?"

"It's what's inside that counts." Victoria crossed her arms over her chest and stared down Serenity who bit her lip to keep from laughing. "And I sense the spirit of a baby goat in Ivy."

Jess couldn't hold in the laughter any longer. When she caught her breath, she said, "Much as I'd love to stand here and debate Ivy's intrinsic animal nature—although I would have chosen lioness—Ivy's right, we do need to get moving. I'm sure we all have busy schedules." With that, they all moved to their vehicles and caravanned to the address Ivy had given them.

—— *eee* ——

THE PARTNERS STOOD IN the middle of the living room after completing a quick walk-through of the vacant house that might become their next project. Though it boasted a choppy floor plan, Jess had no doubt Victoria would wield her creative magic and turn it into a wonderful family home.

"Now that we're here and all alone—with no prying ears other than our own, of course—what's up with you and the dream-worthy Devin?" Victoria asked.

"There's nothing up with me and Devin. We're friends." The last thing she needed was for her partners to suspect Jess' growing attraction to her sexy employee. Her breath hitched and a multitude of wings beat inside her chest. Things were moving too fast but there was something about Devin that made her think home, hearth, and family. She needed to put the brakes on that line of thinking—fast. She had no use for a pile of wishful thinking cluttering her mind. Deep, lasting relationships needed to age like fine wine until trust had a chance to become robust and full-bodied.

Kaitlin arched one brow. "You do remember who you're talking to? I've known you since we were in diapers. The way you were dancing with Devin the other night... that's not just friends."

"And the way their heads were together most of the night..." Ivy let the sentence trail off. Her smirk spoke volumes and had heat rising to Jess' cheeks.

"And don't forget those lingering touches." Victoria fanned herself with her hand. "The air fairly crackled with sexual tension."

"If the woman says they're just friends, then they're just friends." Serenity positioned her body between Jess and the gaggle of honking geese.

If they discovered her plans to see Devin this weekend, she'd never hear the end of it. "Really? You guys are going to go there? You know my policy—no dating employees. No matter how good-looking they are." *Liar. Liar.* The words dug their ugly claws into her conscience.

"So you admit he's good-looking?" Victoria pounced on that admission.

"Of course I do. I'm not blind, but that doesn't mean I have any intention of jumping his bones." Jess sure hoped the flutter in her belly didn't disrupt the sarcastic disinterest she'd aimed for. "Now if you guys don't mind, can we get on with the matter at hand?"

She was met with shrugs all around but the four sets of eyes focused on her all gleamed with speculation. Jess shook her head in exasperation. Time to grab the reins and take control.

"Serenity, why don't you go figure out what you'd propose for the exterior? Victoria, do you need me to follow you around while you decide what structural and cosmetic changes you'd like to make to update the floor plan?"

Victoria shook her head and Jess could see that her mind was already reeling with ideas.

"Good. Then I think the rest of us can get on with our days." Jess snapped the metal clipboard shut. "Can we all meet back at the office at five to come up with some cost projections and make a decision?"

After everyone checked their schedules and agreed, Jess made her escape. Her friends' speculation put too many 'what if' ideas into her head. A big dose of normal was exactly what she needed.

SATURDAY MORNING JESS SAT AT her kitchen table attempting to visualize what her prized possession—her home in which she'd invested so much of herself—would look like to Devin. All the work she'd done so far had been to turn that vision of home in her head into reality—a place that was welcoming, nurturing, and would fold her in loving arms. Inviting him into her space felt risky and made the toast and eggs on her plate less appetizing. But then, wasn't life about taking risks?

Glancing at the clock, she gathered her dishes and placed them in the dishwasher. He'd be here soon and she didn't want to look like a complete domestic flop. A little hot water and soap took care of the skillet. She unplugged the toaster, stowed it in the cupboard and brushed the crumbs it left behind into her palm. After dusting them into the sink, she wiped down the old-fashioned Formica countertops and her kitchen table and straightened the dish towel hanging over the oven door handle.

Pausing, she assessed her handiwork. Satisfied, she made her way to the garage to collect the tools and supplies they'd need for the guest bathroom renovation. She'd just deposited everything to complete today's project in the hall outside the guest bathroom when the doorbell rang. It was an old-fashioned, Victorian bell like in Downton Abbey that she'd searched high and low to find. It's tinkling *ding, ding, ding* never failed to tickle her whimsical side.

Hustling down the stairs, she paused a moment to straighten her shirt and smooth back the tendrils of hair that had escaped from her low ponytail. Jess inhaled to calm the giddiness tumbling about in her belly and opened the door. The giddiness ratcheted up a notch at the hunger in Devin's eyes. He'd seemed so distant when they met. Was that only two weeks ago? She wasn't sure how to handle the attraction sizzling between them, especially since he was her employee. But being with Devin felt right. A rightness that baffled her. She didn't know what it was about him that made her heart beat faster and a soft heat to creep into her cheeks, but she liked it. She shouldn't like it but she did.

"Hi." His voice had a catch in it. Nerves? He bent forward as if to kiss her, then pulled back. Only his breath grazed her cheek.

An ember ignited in her chest. She'd wanted him to kiss her, really kiss her, and she needed to tamp that down. Stepping back, she ushered him in. "Welcome."

He shifted the cloth grocery bag from one hand to the next as he moved to inspect the rooms off the entry hall—living room to the left and dining room to the right. She had a strong urge to fist pump the air at his nod of approval.

"This place is great. I love the wide-plank oak flooring. Nice refinishing job."

"Thanks. Would you believe they'd covered this entry with linoleum?" She clasped her hands together to keep them from waving about wildly.

"No kidding. Why would anyone cover up this beautiful, natural wood?" He crouched down and smoothed his fingers over the floor.

"Beats me, but it was a bitch to get up without doing too much damage to the floor beneath. At least the living room and dining room were carpeted so I could simply rip it up."

He stood and picked up the bag of food he'd brought. "You did all this by yourself?"

"Most of it. I brought in my crew in the beginning to help remove some walls but after that, I've been on my own." She shrugged. "I like it that way. Working on my house relaxes me."

"Well, I'm impressed. I was a little surprised by the outside color. It's very pink."

Heat again crept up her neck. "Someday it will be a pale yellow or cream, but for now it is very pink." She cleared her throat. "Should we put what you brought for dinner in the kitchen?"

"Probably a good idea. I hope you like chicken and vegetable stir fry."

Jess motioned for him to follow her. "I like anything I don't have to prepare." A bubble of pride swelled in Jess' chest when he paused to run his hand over the woodwork framing the opening between the foyer and the great room. She'd spent countless hours sanding off the paint and then refinishing the mahogany beneath. In her opinion, the effect was breathtaking. The light pouring through the transom and glass panels surrounding the front door made the dark woodwork shimmer in the reflected light.

Once they'd made their way into the kitchen he set the groceries on the countertop. "You weren't kidding when you said the kitchen was a..." He seemed to be searching for a politically correct word.

"That's okay. You can say it. Disaster." Worry tightened Jess' throat. "Will you be able to work with this, or do we need to order pizza?"

"If you've got a large frying pan and the burners on the stove work, then I can manage." He squeezed her hand. "Don't look so worried. If what you've finished so far is any indication, once you get around to updating the kitchen, it'll be the envy of the neighborhood."

Relief nearly buckled her knees. She could kiss this guy... so she did. The minute her lips settled on his, her pulse skyrocketed. What she'd meant to be a casual, thank you kiss, turned into steam and sizzle and *oh my God, I'm in trouble*.

# Chapter Seven

BEFORE SHE KNEW IT Jess' backside made contact with the kitchen counter. Hot, hungry lips wiped everything else from her mind. Delightful shivers worked their way down her spine when Devin captured her bottom lip between his teeth and gently tugged. His tongue eased into her mouth and flicked against her own tongue in a tantalizing game of tag. His hands cupped her butt lifting her and pulling her tightly against the bulge in his jeans.

Her legs automatically circled his waist and locked behind his back. He moved forward until her butt rested on the counter. The urge to align her most feminine parts with his erection hit hard and fast. Her breath came in pants. Never had she gone from zero to sixty in a matter of seconds. Her blood rushed hot and wild through her body. She would gladly have lain back on the counter, pulled him on top of her, and done the deed right here in the kitchen. But that protective instinct she wore like a mantle held her back, and she simply clung to him. Let him show his intentions before she gave her body and her trust to him.

His lips moved on to explore her neck, pausing on each area where the nerves gathered to send signals to the brain. The labored puffs of his breathing were the first to mark that tender spot below her earlobe followed by the caress of his lips. Her abdominal muscles contracted in response and her panties grew damp. His enticing mouth and tantalizing tongue slowly worked their way down the column of her neck to focus on the crease where shoulder and neck met. His touch generated a jolt of electricity that tingled throughout her body.

Her fingers tangled in his silky hair then fisted when the fingers of one of his hands traced the contours of her breast. Fire poured through her veins fanned by the winds of desire. When he lifted his head and broke contact, she felt adrift. As though her ship had broken its moorings.

"Jess, I didn't come here today to make a move on you. I really only planned to get to know you better." His breathing sounded like a steam engine chugging up a steep incline. "Your kiss short-circuited my brain." He leaned back and his hands smoothed lightly up and down her arms.

He looked toward the ceiling and drew in a steadying breath. Fascinated, she watched his Adam's apple bob as he swallowed. His hands trembled on her arms as he fought for control, but he didn't step away.

"It's obvious where I want to go with this but you are under no pressure," he said. "I may need a cold shower before we get to work on your bathroom project, however." His tight chuckle sounded like he was pushing air past a boulder obstructing his airway.

Slowly her legs loosened their grip around his waist and she lowered them to the floor as she scooted off the counter. Rising on tip toes, Jess softly kissed his lips and took his hand. She led him out of the room. He didn't ask where they were going. Frankly, she wasn't sure herself until she started up the stairs toward her bedroom. When she reached her destination, a certainty settled over her. She wasn't promiscuous by any stretch of the imagination. So it surprised her how much she wanted to take this step with Devin. She shouldn't, since this would violate one of her rules, but she wanted him more than she wanted anything in her life.

At the doorway to her bedroom, she paused. Common sense a final whisper in her ear. "If you think this will affect our working relationship, tell me now."

"Our working relationship should be fine. You're the boss and the expert." He squeezed her hand and his nod acknowledged her position. "I'm just a simple grunt hoping to learn from the master." Devin smoothed his hand over her hair. "Whether or not we do this, is up to you. If you want to back away and get to work on your bathroom..." He traced her lips with his thumb. "I'll follow your lead."

Any hesitation flitting at the edges of her conscience, evaporated. Gathering the hair on either side of his ears in her fists, she tugged his head down to her level. The kiss roared out of her like a Porsche on the Autobahn. That kiss owned the road and aimed to blow out all the carbon that had built up in her slumbering sexuality. By the time they clutch-walked in the direction of her bed, the blood pounding in her ears made it impossible to hear. She could have stood in the middle of an orchestra's percussion section and she wouldn't have noticed the clash of the cymbals.

"I'm guessing this means yes?" he asked.

"If you're expecting an engraved invitation..." Her breath came in pants. "Yes. Yes. Yes."

Their words mixed on mingled breaths before their lips fused. Her hands groped for the hem of his t-shirt. Finding it, she hooked her thumbs under the edge, and palms flat against his toned abdomen, inched the garment upward until he could fling it over his head. She moaned at the contact her hands made with all the marvelous bare flesh. Muscle definition. Light dusting of hair on his chest. His heart thudding under her touch. Her handful of sexual encounters had been lackluster and provided no comparison.

Devin's hands weren't wasting time either. When the cooler air hit her torso, she realized her shirt had joined his on the floor. Her bra followed in quick succession. They flopped onto the bed, landing on their sides and bouncing. Laughing as their noses bumped with the motion.

Toeing off their shoes, two pairs of footwear landed with a *thunk*. His fingers caressed the soft skin of her stomach as he worked to unzip her jeans. The barriers to skin against skin couldn't disappear fast enough. She lifted her hips so he could slide her jeans and panties down her hips. He eased off the bed, grabbed the hem of her pants and tugged. Finally free of clothing, she stretched her arms over her head, which lifted her breasts, and posed seductively. She delighted at the fire burning in his eyes. The power she held over him became on aphrodisiac. He shrugged out of his jeans and briefs and a surge of desire shot straight to that part of her that longed to be united with that part of him.

He stood there and she watched his gaze travel over her naked body and basked in the approval. Step by panther-like step, he moved toward the bed. The hunter. She shivered in anticipation. Ready for his hands to learn the shape of her body. Ready for his lips to continue to nibble, tease, and tantalize. Ready for him to take her to the moon because she had the feeling that making love to Devin Miller would take her places she had never been before.

"If you're not ready to relegate that delicious body of yours to a higher purpose…" She propped herself on her elbows, "then I suppose we might as well get to work on the bathroom." Feigning nonchalance, she tossed her head letting her thick blonde hair billow around her.

"This body is more than ready to do its duty." He pointed to his erection. "I just wanted a minute to admire you. You're gorgeous." The bed dipped as it absorbed his weight one knee at a time. Straddling her, he swiftly flipped her on to her stomach. "But first I have a little prep work to do."

The sensation of his fingers running feather-light down her spine elicited a primal cry. She tried to flip back over, wanting him inside her but he had a different agenda.

"What's the rush? You have someplace else you need to be?" His husky laughter tickled a place deep inside of her.

"No rush."

His hands stroked up her rib cage. His touch was so gentle it felt soft as lambswool despite the callouses on his palms. "You deserve to be treated like a princess. Pampered. Adored." Her bones felt liquid and languorous. She never wanted these exquisite sensations to end.

"Please, carry on." Her voice hummed with desire. "Your hands are magic." She sucked in a breath as his lips settled on the indentation at the base of her spine and let it out on a whimper. She happily lost herself as his lips worked their way up her spine and his fingers massaged her scalp. She'd never felt so alive.

Handling her as though she were fragile as a hummingbird, he rolled her onto her back. Hands covering her breasts, he lowered his mouth to hers for a kiss that sizzled its way down to her toes. Her hands ranged over the corded muscles of his back now dampened with sweat. The hair on his chest teased her nipples into hard buds.

His erection nestled in the V of her thighs and teased to gain entry. She wasn't sure she could stand much more. She eased one hand between their bodies and gently massaged his balls. He groaned, and she felt his stomach clench against hers.

"If you keep that up, I'm not going to last long," he said.

"Neither am I. If you don't give me what my body demands... right now, I'm going to spontaneously combust... Now is good." Her voice reminded her of sandpaper on wood. "We can always slow things down later."

"Slow and later. I like the sound of that." His tongue circled her nipple and the molten lava inside her started popping and bursting. He positioned himself to enter her and then quickly rolled away and off the bed.

"My wallet. I need my wallet." He snatched his jeans from the floor and tugged his wallet out of his back pocket.

His movements gave Jess a wonderful view of his very nice ass. She giggled as he frantically rummaged through his wallet. He grinned in triumph when he produced a small, flat foil packet. He tore it open with his teeth, rolled it on, and prowled toward her.

"Now where were we?" he asked.

She circled her fingers and slid them down his erection, then gently guided him to her opening. "Right here, if memory serves."

He entered her slowly, filling her, and set a rhythm for an intimate dance. Two people moving in unison to create a beautiful harmony—a perfect oneness. The pressure built, forcing her higher and higher until the air became thin. It seemed as though a river of melted chocolate ran through her veins—warm and thick and turning her insides into a pool of... her mind couldn't find the words. Happiness? Ecstasy? Need? One pebble dropped into a pond and the ripples flow out from the center in a smooth, concentric pattern. Jess' pond just had one hundred pebbles tossed in—in rapid succession. The ripples crashed and crested against each other in a haphazard arrangement until she could barely breathe.

When the pressure could no longer be contained, her world exploded in a clean, white light. Her body expanded and contracted in quick succession. It became hypersensitive—the colors behind her eyes brighter, the scent of Devin filled her nostrils, imprinting him on her brain, the muscles of his back under her fingertips more defined, his groan as he dropped over the cliff with her the only sound she could hear.

So this was what all the fuss was about. Now she understood why sex... great sex... could become addictive.

After they caught their breath, they lay in bed facing each other. His fingers lightly trailed up and down her arm like the brush of a feather and she shivered in delight.

"Who needs a fancy gym workout when sex like this is an option?" Jess smiled at Devin and brought his other hand to her lips. The appreciative look he sent her way set a billion butterflies loose in her stomach.

"I never pictured you as the fancy gym type," he said, his hand coming to rest on her hip.

"I'm not. Everyone plugged into their phones or audio devices. Disconnected from what's going on around them. When I'm out hiking or even at work, I feel like I'm part of something." She leaned in for a slow kiss—nothing hot and heavy—just enough for a satisfying taste. "How about you? Are you a gym guy?"

"No. I'd rather go jogging and lift weights. That feels more liberating than being surrounded by a bunch of other people." He brushed the hair back from her face. "How did dinner with your parents go last weekend? You hinted you weren't looking forward to it."

Jess flopped onto her back. "Buzz kill."

He grinned and kissed her breast. He lingered, giving his tongue time to lavish attention on her nipple.

"Okay, that helps." Her fingers traced his lips when he'd finished with her breast and was again gazing into her eyes. "My relationship with my parents is complicated."

"Aren't they always complicated?"

"I suppose." She sighed trying to decide how much she wanted to share. "My dad wanted a son. He had grand visions of creating a Winters & Sons dynasty. Winters & Daughters didn't have the same ring to it." Jess rolled onto her stomach. She didn't want to look at him. She'd heard the bitterness in her voice and didn't want to see pity in his face. His palm settled on the small of her back. Comforting. Reassuring.

"I can understand why my family is disappointed in me. I was a screw up... but you, you're incredible. You've made a name for yourself." His lips caressed her neck.

"Doesn't make any difference to Dad. I'm still not a boy." A stab of resentment at her father's rejection of who she was and a prick of guilt for never being enough burned under her heart.

"Well, I for one, am glad you're not a guy. He kissed her shoulder. "Otherwise this would be very awkward." If he'd hoped to coax a smile out of her, he succeeded. She shifted on to her back again. Cupping his face between her hands, she pulled him down for a kiss. This pillow talk thing wasn't half bad. She'd expected to feel uncomfortable and awkward afterwards like she had in the past. Wondering what she should do next and fighting the urge to cover herself.

With Devin, she felt at ease. He was a man she could believe in.

She rolled to the edge of the bed and hung her legs over the side. "If you think you're going to tempt me away from today's project with fantastic sex, think again. Time to get to work." Jess stood and sashayed toward the master bathroom. She heard the rustle of sheets and the slap of feet on the wood floor. His hands curved around her waist and he nibbled on her earlobe. Maybe the guest bathroom could wait a little longer.

# Chapter Eight

THEY'D WORKED SIDE-BY-SIDE, MOSTLY in silence, for the last few hours. The result? Stage one of the bathroom update—tiling the walls half way up—was complete. This last month, first working on Bill's crew and now back to Jess', he'd felt useful and needed. For the first time, people counted on him to hold up his end. He still had a lot to learn but was proud of how far he'd come. He had purpose and planned to make the best of it.

Devin stretched his arms over his head to loosen tired muscles, causing his shirt to ride up in the front. He noticed that Jess' eyes zeroed in on his exposed abs so he extended his stretch. Might as well give the lady a show. Amazing what being appreciated did for his self-esteem.

Jess had selected a cream-colored rectangular ceramic tile, topped with two rows of a deep forest green tile, and finished off with a row of bullnose tile in cream. The effect was understated but elegant, as befit the house.

"I like it," Devin said. "Gonna look nice with the flooring tile you picked." He folded his arms over his chest. "I assume the floor is this afternoon's task?"

"It is. I have the tub coming on Monday. Need to get this finished before then."

He noted the look of pride on her face and it made him feel good that he'd played a small role in helping her reach her goal.

"You are planning to break for lunch, I hope?" he asked. "If not, you'll have one grumpy man on your hands." Her chuckle landed square in his heart making it beat a little faster.

"I'm not a total slave driver, no matter what my crew says." She flexed her fingers working out the kinks. "I have sandwich fixings, potato salad, and fresh fruit in the kitchen. Will that tide you over until dinner? Wouldn't want you to die of starvation."

"That'll work." He bent and popped the lid back on the bucket of grout. "Didn't I see a plate of cookies on the counter?"

"Good eye. Yes, that's Kaitlin's weekly care package for which I am eternally grateful." She rinsed and squeezed the moisture out of the sponges they'd used for wiping the tile.

They left the bathroom and started down the stairs. "I don't care how they got here, I'm just grateful for something to feed my sweet tooth."

"A sweet tooth. Something else we have in common. That's why Kaitlin makes sure I'm supplied." The way her slender fingers glided along the handrail fascinated him. He shook himself. He needed to stop daydreaming and start getting her to talk about her dad's business failure.

"So how come you never learned to cook? I gather you've been on your own for a while. I'd think self-preservation would drive you to acquire some skill in that area."

"While we still lived at home, my sister cooked, and I tagged along after my dad." She put her hand beside her mouth in a stage whisper. "My mom is a horrible cook, so it runs in the family." They entered the kitchen. Jess went to the refrigerator and started placing ingredients on the counter. "Besides, there are so many great restaurants. What's the point of making a mess in my kitchen?"

"Your dad didn't mind you tagging along on jobs? I thought he was against women doing construction work?" Devin popped the tabs on the sodas Jess had set out and the sound of their fizz sputtered in room. "Glasses?" he asked.

Jess motioned to a cupboard beside the sink. He retrieved two glasses and filled them with ice.

"When I was little, he thought it was cute. By the time I was junior high, I was free labor." She shrugged and placed silverware and plates on the small, ice cream parlor table in the bump out at the end of the kitchen.

"You didn't mind being taken for granted?"

"Of course I minded."

He heard the edge in her voice and his hand tightened on the knife he was using to spread mayonnaise on the bread. He noticed she tried to make it sound like no big deal but he wasn't buying it.

"I wanted him to see how capable I was. To respect my craftsmanship—still do—but I love the work, so I put up with his indifference." She placed lettuce leaves and sliced tomatoes on a plate and set it on the table beside the plate of turkey, ham, and provolone cheese slices.

Devin piled the deli meat and cheese on a slice of bread, layered it with lettuce and tomato, and topped it with another slice of bread. He bit into his sandwich with a vengeance. "What does your mom think about the way he acts?"

She poured the soda into her glass and he watched the foam creep close to the top. "She loves him." Jess chewed on her bottom lip. "Mom loves me, and my sister too, but he's the one she plans to spend the rest of her life with. She knew we'd leave the nest someday, but my dad would always be there for her." She shredded bits of lettuce hanging over the edge of her bread. "I don't know if that makes sense but that's how I read the situation."

He hated that she wouldn't look at him. It tore at his heart. He'd developed feelings for her. He hadn't intended to, but he knew that was the truth. Still, he needed to keep probing to find out what she knew. "Is your dad still in construction? Which would make you his competitor? I can see why there might be some tense dinner conversations."

She took a deep breath. "No, he lost his business in my sophomore year in high school." She looked away and her hands clenched. "He's been bitter ever since. Anyway, my sister and I keep hoping he'll eventually want to build a bond with us and have kept the door open."

"You're kinder than I am with my father." He sucked in air through his teeth and a heavy lump settled in his stomach. "So how did your dad lose his business?" Again her face closed.

"It's not something I want to talk about right now." She cocked her head and studied him. "I assume from comments you've made that your parents aren't pleased with their... what did you call yourself?" She tapped her head with her finger. "Black sheep? How did you end up with that dubious distinction?"

He hated hedging the truth but until he was ready to tell her why he was here and who his family was, he didn't have a choice. If he couldn't find proof, then none of what his father had done would become public. He suspected she'd be willing to help, but honestly, he wanted to do this on his own. He'd spent too many years depending on others to fix things. Hopefully when all was said and done, she wouldn't hate him for keeping secrets.

"I was a handful as a teenager. My dad sent me to military school, thinking that would straighten me out." Devin sipped his soda hoping that would calm his stomach. "Didn't work. By college I'd started experimenting with prescription drugs and went downhill from there." He paused. "Kaitlin didn't tell you I'd been in rehab?" Even though Kaitlin had said she wouldn't, he'd expected her to have told Jess. It was disorienting to be treated like a person and not an addict.

"No, she didn't. Unless she thought something she learned during the hiring process would impact your work, HR matters are kept private." She touched his arm light as a hummingbird kissing a flower. His body felt the benediction. "But you seem to have come out on the other side of your addiction. Any chance you can patch things up with your parents?"

"My family dynamics are complicated." He needed to steer her away from asking too many questions. Even though Miller was a common last name, he didn't want her to make the connection.

"My sister's the one who got me into rehab. She went to college back East and stayed there." His sister had handled the situation much better than he had. Maybe because she was younger when they learned of their father's dishonesty. Pride swelled his chest. "She's a pharmacist in New Jersey and convinced me that getting away from everything

I knew would make getting clean easier." He moistened his lips and looked Jess in the eye, hoping he wouldn't see repugnance there. She met his gaze with encouragement and a nod to continue the story. He quietly exhaled.

"I'd pretty much hit rock bottom and realized if I didn't shift gears, I'd find myself skydiving without a parachute." He took a bite of his sandwich, chewing slowly to give himself time to think. Reliving the bleakest period of his life wasn't easy. When he swallowed, the food had to make its way past the lump in his throat. "She was right. The change of scenery, getting into rehab, and Madison's—that's my sister's name—constant support gave me a second chance. Been clean for over two years now."

"I'm glad. I know you have to recommit to sobriety each day but the past shouldn't be the sole arbiter of our future." She pulled the plate of cookies closer and snuck one out from under the plastic wrap. "Now that you're clean, where do you see yourself in the next few years? Any big plans?"

"Thought I'd try out a few options first and see what fits. I'd never thought of the future in terms of my life." He snagged a cookie off the plate and took a bite. Peanut butter and chocolate grabbed his taste buds and swung them around. "These are good. Anyway, I discovered the 'Oakland A's' didn't need any pitching talent. Their loss." Her soft laugh warmed his heart. "Tried my hand as a Blackjack dealer at one of the local casinos. Didn't like being inside all the time, and the white shirt and vest…" He shook his head. "Not my style. I'm liking this construction gig, though. Might be a keeper."

"I get it. You plan to take it one day at a time."

He heard the hesitancy in her tone and his chest squeezed. "For now. Drifting isn't my forever position but I want to give myself time and permission to figure out what I love." He wrapped his hands around the glass and the coolness felt good against his palms. "Part of the Program is to look inside and make peace with whatever led us to addiction in the first place. To forgive ourselves. To forgive those who wronged us. To make amends to those we might have wronged. Until I've completed the process, career and other decisions can wait."

He stood abruptly. He'd shared more than he'd planned and hadn't gotten any new information about the reasons behind her dad's business failure. "If we're going to finish tiling the bathroom floor today, we'd better get a move on it." He picked up his plate and glass and carried them to the sink. "I want to make sure I have plenty of time to make dinner. Let you see my sensitive side."

Her face furrowed in a puzzled frown, but he heaved a sigh of relief when she let the conversation drop. No doubt she had questions, and he'd better come up with some good answers.

AFTER LUNCH, THEY PICKED up where they'd left off with the bathroom project and Jess quietly fumed. Why did he clam up or change the subject every time she brought up his family? It was his business what he shared and what he didn't about himself. But they'd made love, damn it, and that meant something to her. She expected him to trust her. Secrets bothered her. Important people in her life had kept secrets from her and she'd gotten hurt in the process. Her father shutting her out. Her college boyfriend had cheated on her and her other serious relationship with a business colleague had ended in disaster. She wasn't going to let that happen again.

An hour later, Jess stood and bent to put a hand on her protesting knees. "Now I remember why I lay flooring in small batches. I have a renewed respect for guys who do this every day." She scooted another box of tiles into the room with her foot.

Devin stood as well and worked his back from side to side. "Want me to cut some more tiles to fit along the edge?" he asked.

"Not yet. I'd like to savor what we've accomplished for a minute." She pointed to the wall by the door. "Victoria found an antique wooden medicine cabinet to hang there." She motioned to the wall with the plumbing stubs. "And I'll have double sinks mounted in a sideboard I found. A framed mirror will go over each of the sinks and some antique-looking lighting. I can't wait to see everything in place."

Devin leaned a shoulder against the wall. "When you finish this, what's the next project?"

"Refinishing the stairs and all the upstairs floors…" She grinned at him. "One room at a time. I tackled the living room, dining room, entry, kitchen, and great room in one fell swoop. I couldn't move for a week afterward. Learned my lesson."

"You don't have to do the work alone. I'd be happy to help. Just say the word." He reached for her hand and squeezed it. "I'm learning a lot."

She smiled at him and the butterflies started up again. "I will." She crouched and busied herself opening the box of tile. "I think my dad's objection to me working in the construction industry goes beyond his belief that women don't belong there." Her palms grew damp and her heart thumped in her chest. She'd never shared what she was about to say except with Serenity. "I know something happened—a bad business deal—and he's been bitter ever since." She sighed "Not that he's ever been the touchy-feely type, but maybe in his own odd way he actually cares about me."

Devin crouched beside her and brushed his lips to her temple. "I hope you're right." He turned away and started pulling tiles out of the box. "Do you know anything about the deal that went sour?"

Jess heard the caution in Devin's voice, and puzzled, eased to a sitting position to put on her knee pads. "Not really. Anyway, I brought this up about my dad because there might be hope for a reconciliation between you and your parents. From what you say, you're not the same person you were when you went away." The darkness flicked across his face so swiftly she wasn't sure she saw it but his next words convinced her she had.

"Sent me away, you mean. Washed their hands of me and didn't look back." He stood. "I'll cut those tiles for the edge now." Seconds later the sound of the tile saw slicing through tile erupted from the hall.

Jess' shoulders slumped as disappointment weighed her down. She'd hoped that by opening up to him, he'd open up to her. He only seemed interested in asking questions about her dad. What was it he didn't want her to know?

# Chapter Nine

"IT'S A PLEASURE TO meet you, Shelly." Devin held his hand out to his brother's wife, a tall brunette.

She grinned at him and instead of accepting his hand, embraced him in a shy hug. "I'm thrilled to finally meet one of Phil's siblings. I was beginning to think he was making you up."

Devin couldn't help but grin back. Shelly had that effect on people. He'd expected someone impeccable and reserved like their mother. Not this down-to-earth woman with a smudge of paint on her hand who exuded sunshine and friendship.

"Now that I'm back in the area, I'm hoping to make up for lost time," He nodded at his brother, "Phil was only seven when I was shipped off to military school, and I'd like to get reacquainted." Devin regretted the choices he'd made that had led to the separation. Part of his rehab meant he had to face the mistakes he had made and try to make amends if he ever hoped to make himself whole.

"But you've been close to Madison. More than I've been able to be." Devin heard the hurt in his brother's words.

"Why don't you two go talk in the living room while I finish getting dinner on the table?" Shelly asked.

Devin didn't miss the '*go make nice*' look Shelly gave her husband.

"You boys take all the time you need. Dinner can hold, and I've got some things to do in the nursery." She placed a hand on her rounded belly.

Devin followed his brother into a tastefully-decorated and inviting room. The L-shaped sofa was covered in a light, blue-green brushed fabric. Two dark brown side chairs sat opposite with a heavy wooden coffee table in between. A river rock fireplace dominated one wall and floor to ceiling windows filled another, opening the space to a huge, private front yard. A large area rug with streaks of brown, seafoam, and cream finished the décor.

"You've done well for yourself." Devin sat in one of the side chairs. Phil wandered over to the fireplace and rested his arm on the mantle. Seemed his brother wasn't quite ready to fully accept Devin. He hoped that would change but he understood Phil's reluctance.

"Business is good. Luckily our firm had enough cash on hand to weather the housing market crash so we came out okay." Devin made note that Phil referred to TLM Investments as 'our firm'. He'd definitely cast his lot with their father. "Sadly, not everyone was so fortunate." His brother's fists clenched but he showed no other signs he was affected. "While I don't agree with Dad's contention that one person's loss is another person's gain, I'm grateful we landed on our feet. With a baby on the way, it's more important than ever that TLM Investments remains successful."

"I'm glad you came out on the upside. But I hear you, too many people lost way too much, and it didn't have to happen." Devin's lips thinned. When he'd been on the streets before Madison got him into rehab, he'd seen the despair of people who had lost their homes, savings, and jobs. This was one of the reasons he was fighting so hard to bring justice to people his father and hurt. In the grand scheme of things it might not be much but it was his small contribution to bringing balance back to the universe.

"Hey, we didn't cause their misfortune." Phil's tone was defensive.

"No, you didn't. Folks thought home prices would only keep going up, and lenders made it easy for them to spend more on a house than they could afford." Devin shrugged. He didn't want to rile his brother. "Like you, I feel sorry for those who were hurt." He lightly grasped his knees and smiled at his brother. "You're going to be a dad. Is that surreal or what?"

Phil's grin spread from ear-to-ear. "Yeah, two more months, and we'll welcome our son into the world. That's one of the reasons we bought this house. Great place to raise our kids."

"Driving in, I saw lots of kids riding bikes and mom's pushing strollers. Seems like just the place for you." Devin got up and walked to the window. "If the backyard is anything like the front, there'll be plenty of room for a swing set, maybe a jungle gym." He turned to Phil who had come to stand beside him. "I always wanted a tree house." Someday when he had his own kids, he'd build one.

"That's funny. Me too." Phil gazed out over the yard and sighed. "Can you imagine Mom and Dad ever letting something as tacky as a treehouse mess up their pristine landscaping?"

"Nope. Their focus was on flash and show—not what might make their children happy." He put his hand on Phil's shoulder and was gratified he didn't shake it off. "If you ever need any help building some play structures for your kids, you let me know."

"I will." He looked at Devin and smiled. "Me wielding a hammer and saw? That'd be a sight."

"Don't sell yourself short. Besides there's no time like the present to shake things up. Did you ever dream about doing something other than working for Dad?"

Phil scrubbed a hand over his hair. "I always wanted to be a high school math teacher."

"Why didn't you do that?"

"Dad paid for my college. Said there was no money in teaching, so I got my MBA instead." Phil's brows creased as he looked at Devin. "If Madison hadn't shunned Dad, he would have paid for her education as well. That wasn't a smart move on her part."

Devin wandered back to his chair and sat. Phil followed and sat in the other side chair. "About Madison... and why she and I are estranged from Dad."

"I'm listening." Phil sat back with his hands resting on the padded arms of the chair. The only sign of tension was the restless drumming of his fingers.

"When we were kids..." Devin rubbed a hand over his eyes. "I was about fourteen, so Madison must have been ten, and you, five or six. Anyway, we were in Dad's office scrounging for the loose change he used to dump in the drawer. We knew he wouldn't give us any money." Devin huffed a breath out through his nose. "Our friends were going out for ice cream, and we wanted to go, too. We knew we shouldn't be in Dad's office, so when we heard him coming, we hid." Devin paused and swallowed. That day rushed back, and his palms grew damp.

"Go on." Phil nodded, but Devin saw his brother preparing for the bad news.

"The phone rang and we heard Dad talking to some contractor. Heard him tell the guy that he could come after Dad if he wanted his money but Dad would bury him in lawyers." Devin blew out the air gathering in his lungs. Even after all these years, it still made him feel ill that their father didn't care—and even seemed to enjoy it—if he ruined another man's life.

"Dad laughed and said, *that's your problem Winters.* He'd pay him whatever he thought the job was worth, and he should be glad to get it. He didn't care what the contract stated, or what the job actually cost the guy. Dad would claim the work was shoddy and ruin the guy's reputation if it ever got as far as a lawsuit." Devin wanted to pound his chest to loosen the lump lodged there. The feelings came flooding back. Anger that his father could be so cavalier about the havoc he caused in people's lives. Fear that bringing the secret to light would hurt his mother and siblings. Shame that he'd taken the coward's way out and said nothing.

"Are you really sure you understood what the conversation was about? You were pretty young and only heard one side of the conversation. The contractor might have been at fault. Maybe the work was sub-par." Phil crossed his arms against his chest.

"Oh, I understood enough to know Dad was cheating this guy. I jumped out of my hiding place and confronted him. He snorted at me and told me this is business and I'd better get used to it if I was going to follow in his footsteps." Sweat popped out on Devin's forehead. The humiliation stung even now.

The man he'd looked up to as a respected member of the community was a crook. He wasn't respected. He was feared. "I told him I'd never cheat people. I'd never be like him. He grabbed my arm and shook me." Devin had to clear his throat again. "Then he told me I'd never amount to anything. I couldn't be his son and must be a mistake and I'd better keep my mouth shut if I knew what was good for me. After that he stormed out of the room."

"What did you do after that?" Phil leaned forward and rested his arms on his knees. Devin watched a muscle tick along his jaw.

"Nothing. As you pointed out, I was a kid, but we started watching him to see if this was a one-time thing. It wasn't. We heard more conversations just like this one. Madison and I talked about it but didn't know what else to do." Devin lifted one shoulder. "We needed an adult to intervene, but other than grandpa, there wasn't anyone who would believe us. Grandpa said it was up to the other person to bring charges if he felt he'd been cheated. We should stay out of it."

"Well, there you have it. Grandpa said it was up to the other guy to do something. Not your responsibility." Phil sat back again but looked more relaxed.

"I could have said something then and I didn't. Maybe no one would have believed me but I should have tried. I knew what he was doing wasn't right." Devin feared his brother was in denial mode and would be ruined if everything collapsed—the firm's reputation in tatters.

"As I've told you before, everything I've seen has been above-board. Sounds to me like what you're saying is sour grapes because Dad sent you to military school to straighten out." Phil shrugged. "I'd need hard facts about these incidents to make a judgement." His face took on a pinched expression. "Now that you're back, do you plan to do anything about your suspicions? Are you planning to cause trouble?"

Devin's gut clenched at his helplessness. "I still don't have any proof that Dad has cheated people. All I've got is what I heard when I was fourteen and the rumors floating around the business community that Dad is not to be trusted."

"You've actually heard people say Dad's not to be trusted?"

"Yes, I have." Devin nodded to reinforce his words.

"I'm not sure I believe you." Phil tapped the arm of the chair with his index finger. "Give me some names."

"Not until people have agreed to go public with what Dad did to them."

"Look Devin, you're my brother and I'd like to take what you say at face value, but you've never been the most reliable guy… at least not in my experience. Maybe you were a Boy Scout once upon a time. Maybe not."

"Understood." Devin nodded and a heaviness settled in his chest. "Most of your life you've only seen me act out and then get hooked on pills. Not exactly a role model or stable influence, but Madison isn't like me, and she thinks Dad is crooked too." Devin reached over and touched his brother's arm. "I'm not asking you to take my word for it, but if I turn up proof, I hope you'll keep an open mind. In the meantime, just be careful."

# Chapter Ten

SUNLIGHT POURED THROUGH THE slats in the upper portion of Jess' shutters. She sat up, yawned, and stretched her arms above her head. Swinging her legs over the edge of the bed, she scrubbed her tangled mess of blonde hair with her fingertips as she walked to the bathroom. On the way, she snagged yesterday's jeans off the back of a chair and rummaged in a dresser drawer for a clean, long-sleeved t-shirt, and fresh undergarments. Someday she'd have closets but those weren't high on her priority list. The armoire would have to do for a while longer. She swiped a finger over the dust-covered furniture. One of the hazards of remodeling... constant dust. She'd get to that chore eventually.

Pulling open the glass door to the shower—her concession to a non-traditional Victorian bathroom—she turned on the water. It took a while for the old pipes to deliver hot water to the second floor. Someday she'd add one of those recirculation pumps to her water heating system so she'd get hot water upstairs faster. She sighed. Another project for another day. A day when the partners were putting more money into their pockets instead of funneling profits into growing the business.

Twenty minutes later, Jess made her way downstairs carrying a can of paint and paintbrushes from last night's project. The guest bath was complete. One item off her never-ending to-do list. She dumped the paint and brushes on the kitchen counter and picked up the stack of mail she'd tossed there when she'd gotten home yesterday. Standing over the trash can, she flicked through the envelopes depositing most of it in the round file. The copy of her industry magazine, she dropped on the kitchen table so she could peruse it while she ate.

She opened the refrigerator and surveyed the contents. Looked like milk and cold cereal were on the menu this morning. She'd meant to stop by the grocery store last night to pick up some eggs, bagels, and sausage. While she didn't have any bragging rights in the culinary department, she could rustle up a mean breakfast when called upon. Unfortunately she'd blazed right on by the store.

Her theme ringtone, "Lips Are Moving" by Meghan Trainor blared from her phone. She looked at the readout. Devin. Her insides suddenly felt as squishy as play dough and even made her cold cereal look good.

"Hi," she said wishing her voice didn't sound like the first *whoosh* of air when the air conditioner started. "Sorry, just rushed down the stairs," she said. Didn't want him to think she was too eager. "Is anything wrong?"

She listened and her mouth curved in a silly grin. The man earned props for saying he simply wanted to hear her voice. She wasn't usually impulsive but the idea that popped into her head charged out like kids on a soccer field. "I'm glad you called. I need an extra man on my crew this morning and you're elected." She looked forward to seeing him again and her foot bounced in anticipation.

After they hung up, the smile remained, as did the feeling she got when the birds sang their little hearts out in the early morning. With a light step, she put her breakfast dishes in the dishwasher, grabbed her clipboard, and jogged to her truck. Today promised to be a good day.

That promise slid into the gooey tar pits of life from which nothing escaped the minute she walked onto the job site. One of her crew was out with food poisoning. Victoria was on her phone arguing with their paint supplier that they'd mixed the wrong color. Finally—at least she hoped it would be the *finally*—the hot water heater had sprung a leak and flooded the garage. Luckily the drywall they would use to finish off the garage had been stack on pallets so hadn't gotten wet. So much for the happy bubble that had surrounded her since her call with Devin.

Resignation settled in. Tackling problems one at a time had help save her sanity in the past. She'd pick up the slack for the employee out sick. She'd planned to visit Bill and Rollo's sites today but that could wait. It'd do her good to get her hands dirty and work alongside her team. Problem one solved.

Victoria hung up her phone, and with her hands on her hips and a Grand Canyon-sized scowl, she faced Jess. She nudged the open bucket of dark green paint with her foot. "On what planet is this color considered pale celery?"

Jess opened her clipboard, flipped to the paint section and retrieved the swatch Victoria had provided when she had the paint mixed. Looking over at Victoria, Jess rolled her eyes. "Jupiter?"

"I'm guessing I'm not going to be painting the bedrooms and hall any time soon so what do you want me to do?" Jamal asked.

"We've decided to finish off the garage. Families like that feature. You can go help Penny with that," Jess said.

"Um," Jamal shuffled his feet. "Penny's not speaking to me right now. Can't Bryan help her, and I'll work on the bathroom tile?"

Out of the corner of her eye she saw Devin enter the room. He stood quietly, watching, with his usual stoic expression. "That wasn't a question. You and Penny will just have to be professional and suck it up." This is why she discouraged workplace romances. She hated having to shuffle her core teams around since most crews developed a working rhythm and the ability to anticipate needs. But if these two couldn't work it out, she would make changes. What would happen if she and Devin had a fight? She fiddled with the watch on her wrist. Could she assign him to another crew? Fire him?

Jamal started to say something, but wisely snapped his mouth shut and left the room. Smart man. She was in no mood for tantrums today.

"About the paint..." Victoria broke in. "They'll make it right, but I'm scheduled to stage a house for Ivy and my crew will deliver the furniture there shortly. I won't have time to go by the paint store until this afternoon."

"Devin will do it." Jess pivoted and handed Devin the original paint order and swatch. "There are two more buckets in the garage. Load them all into your truck and then wait at the paint store until they've mixed the new batch." She touched his arm as he bent to snap the lid back on the open bucket. "And be sure what they give you matches the swatch. We've got to get this painting done today."

"Will do boss." He folded the paper with the paint order and tucked it in his pocket. Then he picked up the bucket and headed for the garage. Problem two solved.

On her way out the door, Victoria called back over her shoulder, "Are you going to get that wall opened today? The inspector will stop by day after tomorrow to sign off on it. Tick. Tock."

"Sure thing." Jess figured the sarcasm in her voice got lost in Victoria's wake.

She pulled her phone out of her pocket and punched in Kaitlin's number. "How soon can you get a plumber out here with a new water heater?" Jess rubbed the back of her neck. "Yeah, I know. Hello to me too. Don't be a smartass. Looks like it's going to be one of those days." When she hung up a few minutes later, problem three solved. She sent up a silent prayer. Please let that be the last.

Might as well make herself useful, and get started on the wall modification in the living room. Swinging a sledge hammer and wielding her power saw might relieve the pressure before it reached the bursting point.

An hour later, Devin found her finishing up the frame for the new arched opening. She'd already removed the wallboard and all but the stud the outlet was on from the new opening and was waiting for the electrician to arrive. Once he finished relocating the existing wiring and outlet, she could finish framing the opening and attach the arch piece. Before the job was complete, they'd need to repair the drywall all around the opening, retexture the wall, and paint.

Jess stepped back purposefully bumping into Devin. She relished the warmth of his solid chest and the reassuring weight of his hands on her shoulders.

"Wish I had the vision that Victoria does," he said. "I had no idea what a difference something as insignificant as opening up a wall would make. Genius." He squeezed her shoulders then moved to stand beside her with his arms crossed against his chest. "Did you do all this by yourself?"

"I did."

He crouched down and examined the wooden arch frame lying on the floor. "You do great work."

"You just figuring that out now?" Jess smiled as pride bloomed in her chest. She did do great work and could hold her own with the best.

His flashed a wolfish grin at her. "No, I figured that out a month ago." He stood and looked at the hole in the wall. "So that arch piece gets attached to the top of the opening?"

"It does, once I've finished off the framing. Then I'll screw it to the new header board. After that I'll nail some thin Masonite to the underside so it's smooth enough to cover with joint compound. Once it's dry, I'll add texture and paint. Have to finish this up before the inspector comes."

"I'll bet Victoria has no idea how much effort her *little change* required." He added some air quotes. "You make it look too easy."

"That's the plan." She glanced toward the thud of footsteps and 'hellos' echoing from the front door. Both the electrician and the cabinet delivery guy had arrived.

"I'm in here." Jess raised her voice to be heard above the tile saw in another part of the house and the *pop pop* of the nail gun in the garage.

The electrician set down his tool box and looked around. "You're making good progress. Didn't expect to be called back out." He grinned. "Victoria throw you another curveball?"

"That she did." Jess glanced at the cabinet delivery guy. "You alone?"

He nodded.

"You need some help unloading?" Jess asked.

"I do. One of our guys hurt his back yesterday, so we're short-handed.

"Devin will help you." She angled her chin toward Devin. "Put the boxes with the kitchen cabinets in the kitchen. All the other sets can go in the Master bedroom until we're ready for them." She looked at Devin. "When you're done, round up Bryan and start hanging the kitchen cabinets."

Devin nodded and followed the delivery guy out the door. Jess showed the electrician where the new outlets would go—a home could never have too many—and left him to do his work. Retrieving her tablet from its pocket inside her clipboard, she fired up her task management program.

The software was one of Kaitlin's innovations. Jess had to admit, it did save precious time. In the past, she'd entered her notes on a checklist by hand, and then someone else would have to transfer the data to the master project spreadsheet. Now the information was in the cloud where they could all access it at any time. To remain competitive, they had to stay up to date with the latest technology. As she wandered from room to room, she checked off the status of the tasks in process. Thankfully, they were right on schedule.

Inspection finished, she followed the sound of male voices. Devin and Bryan leaned against opposite bathroom door jambs and were shooting the breeze.

"Okay you two, I'd like to get the two upper cabinets units hung on the short wall in the kitchen before we break for lunch. Chop. Chop. We don't want to mess with Kaitlin's timeline. I hear there are batches of her famous chocolate chip cookies for each crew that stays on schedule." She bit back a smile when they stood a little straighter. Kaitlin's cooking had that effect on guys. "I'll finish up the tile around the tub while you and Devin tackle the kitchen." She smiled at them to ease any sting in her words. "Bryan, the floor you've done so far looks great. We can set the vanity in this afternoon and hopefully get this floor finished before we leave today."

After lunch Jess enlisted Penny's help to attach the arch frame. She sent Jamal and Devin to continue work on the kitchen cabinet installation. Bryan returned to work on the guest bathroom. She'd also pulled Todd from Bill's crew to help with clean up and to serve as an extra pair of hands where needed. Todd was one of the special employees she'd hired. She'd been asked by the local vocational training program for the developmentally disabled when she'd first started Uniquely Yours if she would consider hiring some of their clients. She believed local businesses should give back to the community and said yes.

Todd was a sweet kid and desperately wanted to please but he didn't always remember the rules. She and Penny were each holding one end of the arch in place and securing it with screws when Todd walked between them carrying a five gallon bucket of paint in each hand. He almost knocked Penny off the step stool she was on.

"Todd, stop," Jess called out more loudly than she intended but adrenaline had increased the volume. He wheeled around and one of the buckets caught Jess in the shin. "Shit," came out involuntarily. "Put those buckets down now." Todd dropped them—luckily the lids didn't pop off—but the poor kid looked like he was about to cry.

Devin rushed in. "What's going on?" He took one look at Todd's face and rounded on Jess. "Don't yell at the kid. He's doing the best he can."

How could he think that after what they'd shared?

Todd wailed, "Oh Miss Winters, I'm so sorry."

Penny's voice added to the din. "Where do you get off telling Jess how to run her job?" She poked Devin in the chest with her finger.

Jamal stood behind Penny looking ready to do battle. Bryan stood off to the side prepared to jump into the fray.

Jess stepped back and raised her hands. "Enough." This time she raised her voice intentionally. Pointing to Devin, Jamal, and Bryan. "You, you, and you. Get back to work." She took a deep breath and lowered her voice. I'm glad you want to defend your co-workers but safety will always come first on my job sites. No one is exempt. But you're going to have to trust that I will always treat everyone fairly. Got it?" Jess looked from one to the other of her employees.

The mutinous expressions were replaced by ones of contrition. "Now, if it's alright with all of you, I'm going to remind Todd about our safety procedures and why they're important."

Each person nodded. "Penny, I'd like you to help Jamal and Devin in the kitchen." Devin's assumption that she'd treat anyone unfairly burned like a hot poker in her gut. Maybe she hadn't been as open as she could have but she thought he knew her better than that.

Devin turned to her before he followed the others out of the room. Leaning close, he whispered, "I'm sorry. I shouldn't have jumped to conclusions. Let me make it up and take you to dinner."

Jess glared at him but he looked so sincere and repentant that she relented. "Okay, but I pick the place."

He stuck out his hand to shake. "I'll pick you up at six-thirty."

Jess nodded then walked over to Todd who still looked stricken and in a gentle voice went over the rules. When she finished, she put a hand on his shoulder. "Want to help me with the arch?" The grin that spread across his face brought the sunshine back into her life.

# Chapter Eleven

THE TANGY AROMA OF Marinara sauce and fresh garlic bread assaulted their senses as they stepped into the small, neighborhood Italian restaurant. Jess had chosen this out-of-the-way diner because it was unlikely they'd run into any of her employees here. Not that she minded her team knowing she was seeing Devin—*they didn't know she was breaking one of her personal rules*—but she wanted to wait until he'd earned his place and his team member's respect. One reason she hesitated to date an employee was to avoid the appearance of favoritism.

While the place was small it didn't feel like a hole-in-the-wall. The owners had taken pains to instill the space with old-world charm. They'd covered the walls with faux brick. Copper pots and pans dangled from wooden shelves and houseplants on the shelves. Wrought iron chandeliers hung from the ceiling. The small, square, wooden tables seated four. Each table was topped with a large votive candle flanked by cruets of olive oil and balsamic vinegar.

After they'd been seated, Devin peered at her over the top of the menu. "Any recommendations? Though I suspect from the smells that everything is delicious."

She lowered her menu. "Truth? I typically close my eyes, stab my finger at the menu, and whatever it lands on, I order." She loved the grin that tilted his lips and brought his dimple out of hiding.

"I like the way you think." He followed her instructions. She hid her mouth behind her hand as she broke out in a severe case of giggles. He looked too darn cute.

The waiter stopped by, took their order, and left a basket of fresh bread on the table. Devin, his eyes cast down, made a show of dribbling the oil and vinegar onto one of the little plates and sprinkling in some of the dried herbs. Jess cocked her head and studied him as he broke a piece of bread in half and, with jerky motions, swirled it in the oil and vinegar mixture. Finally he looked up and stopped fidgeting with the bread.

"About this afternoon, I really am sorry. I know you're not the kind of person to treat someone unfairly. That's not in your nature. I shouldn't have snapped at you."

"So why did you?" Jess waited, folding her arms on the table. "I'm listening."

"You know I was sent to military school." Elbows on the table, he rested his chin on his clasped hands. "Not only was I the new kid but I'd taken to sneaking out and smoking pot. I got the reputation as a pot head, the guy least likely to succeed. I was pretty lonely." He sat back and put his hands on his thighs. "Ever since then, I stick up for anyone who's being picked on."

Jess hoped her smile conveyed how much she respected him. "In my opinion, that's a good trait to have. It sounds like we're each in our own way trying to make the world a fairer place." She took a sip of her water. She wanted to frame her question carefully. "Didn't your parents see how unhappy you were?"

His expression reminded her of storm clouds hovering over the mountains. Thunderous until resignation replaced the anger. "By the time they sent me away, I think they'd written me off as a bad seed. They never visited. Never called." His chuckle held no humor. "My mom did send me birthday cards." He blew air out through his lips. "If Law's family hadn't gotten permission for me to visit them during holidays, I would have been alone."

"Wow. That's pretty harsh." She kept her expression neutral but her insides churned. Her father's indifference was bad enough. She couldn't imagine how she would have coped with being banished. "Who knows the people we would have become if we'd drawn a different set." They both fell silent as the waiter slipped their meals in front of them. "Maybe in the long run, we actually lucked out. Our experiences made us more empathetic to the hardships other people face."

Bending over her plate, she waved her hands over her food and inhaled deeply. If the smell of food could be orgasmic, then this food would definitely send her over the edge.

"If you keep that up," Devin said, "I'll have to go take a cold shower." He glanced at the customers sitting around them. "And I won't be alone."

She felt heat creep up her neck and into her cheeks. Was there a hole she could crawl in? "Sorry," came out on a squeak.

Devin's rumbling laugh spiraled straight to her core. She might have to race him to that shower.

"Since we're sharing hot button issues, the reason I'm such a stickler for safety is that one of my dad's crew... a man who never failed to treat me kindly and who I idolized... was badly injured in an accident." Jess halved a piece of ravioli with her fork and placed it in her mouth. She felt the accustomed sinking feeling in her gut and her meal lost some of its luster as the memories crowded in. She swallowed past the lump. "The accident never should have happened. It was totally preventable but my dad said that's just part of construction. People get hurt."

"I'm glad you don't agree with him. It shows how much you care about your employees."

"I do care about them. They're like family. I've seen how an accident like that can change someone's life. Fred's leg was never the same. He had to get out of construction. He and his wife sold their home and luckily the proceeds were enough to buy a hardware store in Montana." She sighed. "I really missed him."

"Looks like we both came up short in the parent department." Devin picked up his glass of iced tea and raised it in a toast. "To happier topics."

"Amen to that one." She clinked her glass against his.

"Anything new on the horizon?"

"As a matter of fact, we just closed escrow on some land for our new office building. I planned to announce it to the crew tomorrow, so act surprised when you hear the news." Jess felt exhilaration bounded by a frigid dose of apprehension. She really hoped they weren't walking into a quagmire.

"No kidding. Congratulations." He clinked his glass to hers again. "Tell me about it."

"It's in a mixed-use neighborhood east of downtown. Right off highway 50." Excitement fluttered in her chest along with that persistent sense of unease she couldn't seem to shake. "We'll finally get to build what suits our business and we won't be trapped in that boring business park anymore."

"From the look on your face, I'm guessing there's something about this deal you're not happy with?" He reached over and ran his thumb across the top of her hand.

"Yeah." Worry shifted from a hint to a bright warning flag as she vocalized her concerns. "We bought the property from TLM Investments and part of the deal is that Uniquely Yours will do a complete make over on a residential property he owns."

Devin's fork clattered against his plate. "Sorry."

Jess watched a muscle work along his jaw. What was that all about?

He cleared his throat. "I've heard that company has a kind of sketchy reputation. Is that why you're worried?"

"Since you haven't been back in the area long, I'm surprised you've heard of them." Jess noticed how tightly his hands gripped his knife and fork. Odd reaction. "Do you have some history with that firm?"

His grip eased on his utensils. "Several years ago, Law explored working with them. He wants to expand his business to Sacramento and they had some interesting properties. He backed away when they tried to change the terms of the contract after they'd reached an agreement."

"I've heard they try and pull stuff like that—at least the old man does. Haven't heard much about the son." Jess took a sip of her iced tea and welcomed the cool liquid on her dry throat. "Anyway, Ivy has dated a top real estate attorney and he drew up the contract. The owner has to pay after each stage of the project is complete—and we made those stages very limited in scope—so if he tries to stiff us, we won't be out much. None of us trust the guy and are going in with our eyes open."

"Given Law's experience, that seems prudent. If the guy has such a bad reputation, why do people keep doing business with him?" Devin asked as he spooned the last bite of his meal into his mouth.

"Some of his business practices are questionable. Those of us who've been in construction in this area for a long time, have learned to approach deals with him with caution." Her teeth worried her bottom lip and she grimaced before she spoke. "I've heard about a few contractors who've filed lawsuits against him years ago, but nothing ever went to trial that I know of."

She watched him sit up straighter. "Really? Who?"

Jess rattled off a few names, and he seemed to be filing them away in his mind. "Why so interested?" Another muscle jumped along his jaw and she had the impression he willed himself to relax. The smile he produced looked normal enough.

"I don't know. I guess I'm just an old gossip." He put his napkin on the table. "What do you say we order dessert to go and get out of here?"

Jess snorted. "You? An old gossip?" She placed her napkin on the table as well. "Sure. I'm ready to leave. They make a great tiramisu. How about we order that?"

"You haven't steered me wrong yet." He raised his hand to get the waiter's attention.

"My house?" she asked.

Devin nodded. "I won't be in a place of my own until the first of the month so that's what I was hoping."

After they paid and collected their dessert, he walked her to her truck. His hand at the small of her back sent a slow burn up her spine. Desire swirled in her core and her nipples tightened. Maybe the tiramisu could be the follow-up dessert. She didn't want to make a habit of asking him to stay the night but her resolve to stick to her rules crumbled when Devin was around.

# Chapter Twelve

HE BANGED HIS FIST against the steering wheel as he followed her tail lights. James Bond he wasn't. The last thing Devin wanted to do was arouse her suspicions. He'd been too eager when she mentioned she'd heard about some lawsuits and almost given himself away. He could only imagine what would happen if she found out he'd been keeping secrets. She hated secrets.

So far, he'd gotten nowhere with his public records search. He'd searched online and made a few visits to the courthouse after he'd gotten off work. No lawsuits. No liens. Not even a complaint to the Better Business Bureau. The lack of filings would make a person think TLM Investments was squeaky clean. Devin knew better. Knew in his gut his dad was dirty.

Now that he had some names—names she had unwittingly sup-plied—maybe he could turn something up either in the public records or by talking to the people involved. One of them might be willing to talk. That might not work though. If they hadn't gone through with their lawsuit, they might not want anyone to know what had happened—or more likely, his dad had paid them off to keep quiet. Whatever he did, he'd have to be careful. He couldn't risk word getting out too soon regarding his suspicions about his father's shady, and probably illegal, activities. Not until he'd figured out a way to protect his brother from the fallout.

Scrubbing a hand over his face, Devin tried to put it all out of his mind. He was so far out of his element. He'd see Law Saturday morning and he might have some ideas. Shaking his head, he had to wonder what was wrong with him. He was following a gorgeous woman to her home, and unless he was way off base, she had more on her mind than sharing dessert with him.

The image of Jess naked and waiting for him had the desired effect. When all his blood rushed south, his brain short-circuited. He slammed on his brakes, realizing that the light had turned red while he day-dreamed. His body hummed with anticipation and his heart beat faster. *Come on light... change.* As soon as it did, he stepped on the gas and shot through the intersection. Glancing at his speedometer, he eased up on the gas. A ticket wasn't in his budget, and a delay in reaching his destination wasn't on his agenda. Jess. He needed to be with her. He yearned to touch her and to feel her soft hands on him. He'd never felt such a powerful attraction before and desperately wanted to explore where it would go.

He pulled up to the curb and stepped out of his truck. She stood on the front porch rummaging through her backpack. Her blonde hair glowed under the porch light. She must have heard him arrive because she gave him a sideways look and dangled the keys from her fingers. Even though she took his breath away, most people probably wouldn't describe her as beautiful. Attractive? Yes. Curves in all the right places? Yes. Cute. Yes. Ready smile. Yes. She'd fit right in dressed in a short cheerleading skirt and pom poms. Now there was an image his imagination could latch on to.

But there was that other side. She had a sharp edge, earned he was sure, by holding her own in what was conventionally considered a man's world. His lips curved up. Jess and conventional would rarely occur in the same sentence. She wasn't one to back down or behave the way a certain subset of men expected her to. She ran a tight, but fair, ship. She knew her stuff. Had worked in the construction industry most of her life. She'd studied construction management and best practices in college. Her competence and integrity might intimidate some men. But not Devin. With every fiber of his being, he wanted to spend the rest of his days with Jess. He sighed. Too bad dreams were for other people.

When she crooked her finger and made a come-hither motion, his feet sprouted wings and he flew up the walkway. Following her into the house, he nudged the door shut with his foot and leaned against it. Arms circling her waist, he pulled her snugly against him and lowered his lips to meet hers. Electricity spiraled down his body like a corkscrew. Her soft breasts pillowed into his chest just below his heart. She opened her mouth. His tongue slid along hers, tasting the hint of tomato on her breath.

Her hands eased up his arms. The friction of her fingers, sliding over the cotton of his long-sleeved shirt, sent shots of adrenalin down his spine and reminded the bulge in his pants of the pleasure to come. The bag holding their dessert bounced against her butt, and she giggled.

"Maybe we should take this into the kitchen?" she said.

The words softly spoken against his lips must have disrupted his hearing and his ability to process language. "Do what?"

She lowered one of the hands that had been tangled in his hair, reached around her back, and latched on to his hand holding the bag. A determined tug brought his hand into view. "Dessert. Kitchen."

He missed having both of her hands in his hair. They'd been working magic there. Fisting, tugging gently, her fingers lightly massaging his scalp as she positioned his head to deepen the kiss. And his hand that she'd pulled away had been busy cupping her first-class ass—or at least had been trying to. Now he understood why he hadn't gained purchase. Bag. Had to get rid of the bag. His primitive brain—so focused on kissing her until he drew his last breath—couldn't get his thoughts in any kind of logical order. His confusion must have been written across his face in neon letters.

Laughing, Jess stepped aside, took his hand, and led him into the kitchen. Opening the refrigerator, she pointed from the bag he was holding to one of the shelves.

"I get it. If I deposit this," he held up the bag, "there," he tilted his chin toward the refrigerator, "then I'll have two hands free to touch your delectable body. Good plan." With the encumbrance out of the way, he moistened his lips with his tongue. Time to make good on his promise.

His hands slipped under her shirt and up her back. Soft, smooth skin, cool beneath his palms. Her full lips moved against his beckoning him to intensify the kiss—an invitation he eagerly accepted. Inhaling her hum of satisfaction, the bubble of desire expanded in his gut pushing him closer to the edge of control. He'd never felt a connection like this with any other woman. She was a first for him. Unique and alluring.

The tip of his tongue mapped the lush contours of her lips before sinking in for another taste. The desire to explore every inch of her mouth, her face, her body was all consuming. His body vibrated to the beating of her heart against his chest. "Jess, I'm beginning to think I can't live without you. I want you in my life all the time."

"I feel the same way. I didn't think I could feel this way about someone so quickly." Her words, whispered into his mouth, filled his heart. He hadn't meant to express his love and hadn't expected anything in return, but what he said was true.

He traced a line down the column of her neck with the tip of his tongue. His teeth nipped at the crease where her shoulder and neck met. She groaned which pulled an answering groan from him. The feel of her fingernails lightly raking down his back had a thin sheen of sweat popping out on his forehead. His breath came in gulps. His erection thickened and pulsed.

Banging. Banging slowly penetrated the blood pounding in his ears. And the insistent chiming of the doorbell as though someone was stabbing the button repeatedly. Jess lifted her lips from his earlobe where she'd been wreaking havoc with his equilibrium. She must have heard it as well so it wasn't his imagination. He wanted to curse and rail at the gods for disrupting his universe.

"What in the world..." she said. Her forehead wrinkled and frustration filled her eyes.

"Jess. Jess. Are you here?"

Jess stepped quickly away on unsteady legs, rearranging her clothing as she moved. "In the kitchen, Hannah." She put her hand beside her mouth and whispered. "My sister." She smoothed her hand down the front of his shirt, confusion tinged with concern on her face. "She never comes by without calling to make sure I'm at home."

A dark-haired woman, slightly taller than Jess entered the kitchen trailed by an unremarkable-looking man. Her husband? Jess said her sister had recently gotten married. When she caught sight of Devin she stopped short and the man bumped into her. "Oh. I didn't know you had company." She shook her head and threw up her hands. "Doesn't matter. Dad's in the hospital."

"What? What happened?" Jess' hand went to her throat.

Devin stepped up behind her and grasped her shoulders, offering a reassuring squeeze. It may not be much but was all the support he could give her at the moment.

"The doctors don't know for sure yet. They're running tests. He was dizzy and nauseous and has a lot of pain in the stomach area. Could be any number of things."

Her sister turned into the embrace of the man she was with and buried her head for a minute. Jess walked over to her and wrapped her arms around her, resting her head against Hannah's back.

Helplessness washed over Devin along with an uncomfortable awkwardness. He didn't know what to do or how to feel about the situation. Sympathy for Jess for sure. He knew she wasn't on the best of terms with her dad, but he also knew she cared about him. The sisters seemed close. Maybe he should just excuse himself and let the family get on with what it needed to do.

Hannah seemed to gather herself and turned out of her husband's arms. Jess stepped back and wiped a tear from her cheek. Devin's heart thudded in his chest.

"How's mom?" Jess brushed a hand over her hair. "Is she at the hospital?"

"She's worried, and yes she's at the hospital. We need to get back. I don't want to leave her alone too long." Hannah gave Jess a puzzled frown. "I tried calling but only got voice mail. Is something wrong with your phone?"

Jess grimaced, and Devin could feel the tension snapping in the air. Guilt is a bitch.

"It must still be in my truck. It was almost dead, and I was charging it on my way home." She glanced at Devin and he could see the color tinging her cheeks. "I guess I was distracted and left it there."

Hannah pinched her lips together then her face softened into a sympathetic smile. "Sorry for the interruption but I knew you'd want to be there." She stuck out her hand to Devin. "Hi, I'm Hannah, Jess' sister." She patted the arm of the man standing beside her with her free hand. "And this is Bob, my husband."

"I'm sorry to meet you under these circumstances. I'm Devin." He figured it was best to leave how he and Jess knew each other vague. Jess could fill in whatever details she wanted to. Turning to Jess he added, "Look, I'm going to be on my way, unless you want me to come with you."

"No, now is probably not the best time to introduce you to my parents. I'll talk to you tomorrow and let you know what's going on."

"Call me if you need anything." She nodded and he bent and gave her a quick kiss on the forehead. He felt badly leaving her, but she was right, a hospital was not the best place to meet the new boyfriend. Turning, he headed for the door while Jess collected what she would need for long hours at the hospital.

THE ANTISEPTIC SMELL ASSAULTED Jess' senses the instant she stepped through the door to the emergency department. As she followed Hannah and Bob past the reception desk, the next thing she noticed was the controlled chaos whirling around her. Phones ringing. Paramedics wheeling patients in on gurneys and parking them along the walls. Nurses and doctors assessing the urgency and type of care required. Orders firmly communicated. Attendants scurrying to carry out those orders. Equipment beeping. People crowded around the reception desk. Conversations—confused, worried, insistent—circling the room like rambunctious children. The nurses manning the counter took it all in stride. Jess was sure glad Hannah and Bob knew where they were going.

She spotted her mom in one of the exam rooms. The sight of her, pale and tense, slammed Jess with the force of a professional wrestler hitting the mat. Her typically self-assured mom looked small and helpless. When Hannah, Bob, and Jess crowded into the small room, she reeled from her second shock. Her mom had blocked the view of her dad. Seeing him lying in the bed—an IV in his arm, wires tethering him to a monitor displaying fluctuating lines, a bag for urine dangling off the side of the bed, his face contorted in pain—this was not her strong, domineering father. She didn't know how to react.

Jess slipped an arm around her mother's shoulders and hugged her to her side, resting her head against her mother's. "Have the doctors come up with a diagnosis yet?"

"They'll be taking him for a CT scan soon but suspect kidney stones." Darlene gently clasped her husband's hand and took a deep breath. Jess felt the shudder as her mom exhaled.

Gerry squeezed his eyes shut and groaned. "Those pain meds aren't working," he growled.

"Should we see if they can up the dosage?" Jess asked. It killed her to see her dad weak and vulnerable.

"What do you take me for? Some kind of namby-pamby that can't take a little pain?" Her father's words were forced out through gritted teeth.

"No, I know you're tough. If you're hurting, it would probably crush someone else." Jess was relieved to see a mollified expression replace the scowl on her dad's face. "It'd make us feel better if you were more comfortable."

Gerry grunted and brought his arm up to cover his eyes. "Why do they keep it so bright in here?"

"Do you want me to see if I can dim the lights, Dad?" Hannah asked.

"Do I need to draw you a picture? Yeah, if you can figure it out, do it."

Dad hadn't lost his touch. Jess didn't miss the flash of anger on Bob's face or the restraining hand Hannah placed on his arm. Jess kept her face neutral but cringed inwardly.

Darlene patted her husband's arm. "Dear, Jess and Hannah are just trying to help."

Racking her brain for a topic of conversation that would distract him and maybe soften his mood, Jess blurted out the first safe topic that came to mind. "I ran in to Jack Bailey a few days ago. Remember him?" Jess rested her hands on the bed rails, the metal cool under her palms.

"Course I do. I don't have dementia." Gerry glanced up at his wife when she cleared her throat. "Sorry. Yeah, I competed with the guy for jobs for twenty years. Usually beat him, too." Gerry's hand went to his stomach and his face paled. Darlene lightly stroked his forehead with her fingertips.

Jess' nails bit into her arm. Her dad was in pain. She needed to cut him some slack. Yes, his words hurt and her safe topic seemed to have skidded off the rails but keeping him distracted was still a good idea. There was always the chance that a kinder, gentler side would make an appearance. Right. Jess snorted. That would be when her fairy godmother stopped by to sprinkle fairy dust on Jess and turn her into a princess.

"What was that for?" Gerry growled at his daughter and attempted to come up on one elbow. Darlene gently pushed him back down, narrowing her eyes at her daughter.

"Sorry Dad. I was trying to hold back a sneeze. Anyway Jack said to say hi and that the two of you should get together for a beer sometime. He'd like to catch up and talk about old times."

"Damn lumpy bed." Her dad struggled to shift positions. "I'll bet he would, so he can lord it over me about his success. I'm sure he got a good laugh when I had to downsize."

"I didn't get that feeling at all. He's retired now, too. I think he misses his old pals and talking shop." Jess turned her head so only her sister would see the *bail me out* expression on her face. Hannah had a knack for smoothing the waters.

"Didn't you and the Baileys use to hang out? I remember camping trips we took with them. Good times. I'm sure that's all he meant," Hannah said.

With a groan Gerry pressed more deeply into the bed. "If you say so."

"I agree with Hannah. That's all he meant," Jess said. "No one cares about your company's problems. Like you always say, construction is a tough business. Get over it." She was done coddling his ego but she didn't miss her mother's frown.

Gerry scowled at her. "You're all high and mighty now but one of these days something will happen... maybe you'll get married and have kids. Then how will you run your business?" He snickered. "Probably end up marrying some sissy guy who will stay home and be a housewife so you can wear the pants."

"Honestly Dad. I'll do what lots of working couples do. We'll figure it out." She rubbed her stomach. Had someone macrameed her intestines?

"What have you got against Jess?" Hannah asked.

The set to her sister's shoulders had gratitude replacing some of the anger burning in Jess' chest. Her father drove her nuts. Yes, he hadn't taken it well when he lost his primary breadwinner status. He'd hated being reduced to operating a handyman business and having Darlene take a bookkeeping job to make ends meet. Too bad. Lots of people had to deal with adversity. That didn't mean they had to turn bitter.

"Okay you girls, leave your father alone," Darlene said.

At that moment the techs slid open the glass door and stepped into the room. "Mr. Winters, are you ready to get your CT scan?"

"Yeah. Get me out of here."

Jess stood in the hall with her mom, sister, and brother-in-law and watched the techs wheel her dad away. "Mom, why do you always take his side over ours?" Jess' emotions needed a place to go or she'd burst.

"He's my husband." Her mother's words came out clipped. Darlene sighed. "He's had a hard time, and your success is like waving a red flag in front of a bull. You're everything he thought he would be. Life didn't turn out that way."

"But shouldn't he be proud of me?" Jess heard the pleading in her own voice and cringed. "I get that there was some bad luck. Maybe some poor business decisions. That stuff can happen to anyone." Fueled by frustration, the words tumbled out. "Why isn't he proud of me? Why isn't he proud of the woman I've become? I work hard. I built a good reputation. I try to do right by my family." She huffed out a breath. "He sure doesn't make it easy."

Darlene placed a hand on Jess' shoulder. "Sweetheart, that's the way he is. We just have to accept it."

Hannah rolled her eyes.

That was it in a nutshell. Her dad wasn't going to change, and her mom was going to back him up. Jess exhaled releasing some of the frustration. No point beating a dead horse. "What's say we go to the cafeteria and get some coffee while we wait?"

# Chapter Thirteen

THE MID-MORNING SUNSHINE PROMISED another absolutely gorgeous early October day. Jess stepped away from her crew and peered out the kitchen window into the backyard. This was the kind of day that usually had Jess dreaming about a hike in the nearby Sierra Nevada range. The Lake Tahoe area—one of her favorite destinations—beckoned with its soothing vistas and magnificent trails. Instead, a malaise hung over her, drenching her spirits like the victims of a sudden downpour. She couldn't shake the hurtful words her father had used to tear her down. Even seeing Devin again hadn't lifted her mood.

She did what she always did after an encounter with her father—threw herself into her work. The last few hours, she'd helped finish the installation of the new kitchen cabinets. They'd position the island this afternoon and start on the flooring. According to Kaitlin, the supplier had discovered a crack in the piece of granite they'd picked for the countertops, so delivery would be delayed a few days until they could replace it. That had meant rearranging the project work order so they could stay on schedule, further souring Jess' mood. Stuff happened in construction. She knew that, but time was money, and now that the firm had purchased the lot for their new offices, the pressure was even more intense.

Tired of dodging all the concerned glances from her crew, Jess used the pretense of checking on Serenity's progress with the landscaping to get away from the prying eyes. The team could finish without her. They hadn't been obvious, but Jess could feel the questions lurking on the tips of their tongues. They'd heard about her dad and wanted to know that their boss was okay. No one asked outright—choosing to give her space—but everyone was a tad more solicitous than usual. It irritated her that her restlessness impacted her team.

Stepping into the backyard, Jess removed her safety helmet and tucked it under her arm. The crew groused when they had to wear them. Other residential remodeling companies didn't require their workers to wear them, but Jess was firm. Anytime they did work where something might fall on them or they could hit their heads—like installing today's cabinets—they'd protect their heads or could find someplace else to work. Baseball caps didn't cut it.

Her gaze swept the yard. The landscaping was starting to take shape. Serenity had recruited a couple of her college-aged cousins to construct a pergola in one corner and they would lay a flagstone patio underneath it. The sound of hammering paired with power saws and the pop of nail guns calmed her frazzled state. Normal. Jess needed more normal.

Serenity's daughter, Reanna, knelt beside several glazed ceramic pots. The young girl carefully planted bright yellow marigolds in each of them. Once the patio was complete, those pots would provide pleasing spots of color against the patio furniture that Victoria would bring in. Jess wandered over to where Serenity was digging holes in the flower bed she'd created along the north side of the house. The calla lilies and ferns that would occupy that space waited in their plastic containers nearby.

"Reanna doesn't have school today?" Jess asked.

"No. It's a teacher development day." Serenity leaned the shovel against the wall of the house and removed her gardening gloves.

"They sure do have a lot of those. I feel cheated. We never got days off like that."

"Tell me about it. Luckily I have a boss," Serenity pointed to herself, "who's very flexible about letting me bring my child to work. I feel for parents who have to scramble to figure out childcare for these miscellaneous days."

"She looks like she's having a good time."

An affectionate smile spread across Serenity's face as she gazed at her daughter. "She's a good kid. It also helps that my cousins spoil her rotten. I've seen them slipping candy to her all morning. The joys of being part of a large, extended family."

"I don't envy you the sugar high this afternoon." Jess grinned at her friend. "You planning on leaving early today?"

"You read my mind." Serenity dusted her hands on her jeans. "How's your dad?"

"Ornery but coming home later today. Thank heavens the doctors expect him to be able to pass the kidney stones on his own, so he doesn't need surgery." Jess turned her back to Serenity and gazed across the yard.

"And how are you doing?" Serenity stepped close enough to nudge Jess with her shoulder.

Jess made a scratchy sound in her throat and scrubbed her scalp with her fingernails.

"That's about what I figured." Serenity's chuckle held no mirth. "Want to talk about it?"

Jess shook her head slowly. "No matter what I do. No matter how well-respected our company becomes, I'm never going to measure up. He's never going to respect me. In his mind I'm bound to fail."

Serenity tapped the side of her index finger against her lips for a few seconds. "I think deep down you know that's the problem. He can't accept that you succeeded where he failed." She pointed her finger at Jess. "And you've managed to do this by putting your clients first, never chasing the quick buck, never cutting corners. Always ethical. You don't know any other way to be." Serenity pressed her lips together. "I hate to say this, but we both know your dad's business took a hit because he got involved with something too good to be true and lost his shirt."

Jess laced her fingers behind her neck and gazed up at the puffy, white clouds drifting by. If only life could be so carefree. "He's never been the same. I may never know exactly what happened, but I'm sure Thomas Miller did something. I may have to do business with him but I'll never forgive him." A lump clogged her throat and she blinked to keep the threatening tears at bay. "It's hard to swallow that my dad is jealous of what I... what we've built... I don't' know why I continue to hope he'll change, but I do."

Serenity slipped an arm around her and rested the side of her head against Jess'. "Because that's who you are. Generous to a fault. I think fate saddled you with that cranky old coot because you're strong and solid, and while it hurts, you'll keep on going. You're an amazing woman, no matter what your dad says." She squeezed Jess's side. "It's something he can never be... amazing I mean, not the woman part... which we know he won't be." She waved her free hand in the air. "You know what I mean. Your dad will never be a kind and caring person."

"I get what you're saying." Jess pinched her nose. "Funny though, I do remember a time when I was in grade school, when he *was* everything I expected a dad to be. Hannah was too young to remember but he played with us and let us help him build things. He was patient. Gradually when I was around twelve, he had less and less time for us. Too busy working." Jess breathed slowly letting her mind wrap itself around the contradiction.

"Or trying to save his business." Serenity gave Jess a quick hug.

"At the hospital last night, Mom said we have to accept him for who he is. I'm not sure I agree because he wasn't always like he is now."

"I don't often agree with anything your mom says about your dad, but I agree with her on this. When bad things happen, some folks just don't have the strength to fight their way back to their former self. I'm afraid your dad is one of them." Serenity stepped away and picked up her shovel again. "At some point you'll have to come to terms with that and believe in yourself. That you are enough, no matter what anyone else thinks."

"My brain gets it, but my heart's still in denial."

Serenity patted Jess' arm. "But just think, if you weren't constantly trying to prove something to your dad, you wouldn't be the little over-achiever we all love and admire."

A pair of arms wrapped around Jess' legs and a small head burrowed into her belly. "Auntie Jess. Did you see the flowers I planted?"

"I did. They're beautiful. I'm so glad you got to help your mom today." Jess winked at Serenity. "She needs all the help she can get." She framed Reanna's face with her palms, bent down, and rubbed her nose against the young girl's. "What do you say when we break for lunch, we go get hamburgers?"

"And a milkshake?" Reanna grinned up at her mom who rolled her eyes.

"Of course. Can't have burgers without a milkshake." Jess patted the top of Reanna's head before the youngster scampered off.

"I came out here under the pretense of getting a status update, so I guess I better get a report. How's it going?" Jess asked.

"New sprinkler and drip system is in. The guys will finish the pergola and patio tomorrow."

Jess interrupted. "Why aren't your cousins in school?"

Serenity shook her head. "The university system has some lame-ass break this week. Something about reading time."

Jess laughed. "And you're not holding their feet to the fire and making them read?"

Right. Like those guys are going to spend a beautiful October week reading? I'll make sure they get their assignments done, just not today." She shrugged. "Anyway, I'm happy to put them to work and keep them out of trouble. Continuing on, the plantings will be finished today. Sod will be installed day after tomorrow, which gives everything a few weeks to root before this house is put on the market." Serenity slipped her gloves back on. "That is, if I get back to work." She angled her chin toward the back door. "Looks like you have company."

"AH, SHIT." BRYAN, THE senior member of the crew, muttered after he unwrapped the final door for the section of kitchen cabinets they just mounted on the wall. "Can you believe the scratch on this one? We're not going to be able to use it."

Devin set the door in his hands across the sawhorses. He took a closer look at the three he'd removed from that same box and were waiting to be fastened to the cabinet frame. Picking each one up, he checked both sides before he moved over to examine the main unit. "These doors all look fine, and so does the frame. Must be just this one that's damaged."

"We'll still have to put all these doors back in the box they came in, along with the wrapping, and then take pictures of everything including the outside of the box. It doesn't look damaged, so the scratch must have happened at the factory." Bryan rubbed his neck. "We'll also have to check all the other pieces that we haven't unwrapped yet that came in with this shipment. Damn." He took the door from Devin that he had started to rewrap. "Look, I'll do this while you go out and tell Jess. She'll want to see the damage and call the supplier."

"Why am I elected to be the bearer of bad news?"

Bryan grinned. "Because you have the lowest seniority."

"That and the boss has a soft spot for you. The mood she's in today, she'd probably take the head off any of the rest of us. You, on the other hand, might survive." Jamal raised his voice to be heard over the power drill Penny was using. He balanced a two-door cabinet frame on his shoulder and held it flush to the wall with his free hand while Penny stood on a step ladder to screw the unit to the wall.

"Okay. I'll take one for the team." Devin bit his cheek to keep from smiling. He'd seen the speculation in his coworkers' eyes and didn't want to toss any fuel on the fire. With a dramatic sigh, he made for the door, feet dragging and head down like he was off to the gallows. A rag hit him in the back and everyone laughed.

Once he'd cleared their line of sight, his pace quickened. A few minutes alone with Jess... he'd take what scraps he could get and offer what comfort he could. She'd told him on their morning call about what her dad had said to her last night at the hospital. It made him spitting mad. Maybe the guy didn't deserve justice and should continue to feel the impact of what Devin's father had done to him. He flexed and unflexed his fingers. Well, even if Jess' dad didn't deserve it, others did. He'd keep on digging. As he stepped into the backyard he saw Serenity's daughter scurry away from Jess and Serenity toward the group of guys putting together a wooden trellis-like thing.

Jess glanced his direction, and the way her face shifted from dejected to delighted made him feel like he was walking on a bouncy mat. He removed his safety helmet and ran his fingers through his hair hoping to tame the wild, sweaty mess. As much as he wanted to sweep Jess into his arms, feel those womanly curves sink into his body, and devour her with his lips, he wouldn't.

His step faltered when it hit him that what he said to her Saturday was true. He'd fallen for her. He wanted more than *a booty call*. He'd never had a relationship with a girl in high school or college where he'd simply held hands with her. Stole sweet kisses. Cuddled on the sofa and watched a movie together. His lifetime of hookups—because that's all they'd ever been—had only amounted to satisfying needs and moving on. With Jess, he craved a deeper connection. Stopping in front of her, he held his helmet in both hands to keep them from reaching out.

"I'm the sacrificial lamb sent out to let you know we have a slight problem with the cabinet delivery." He grinned when Serenity snorted.

"You look more wolf in sheep's' clothing set to devour the innocent maiden than a sacrificial lamb."

It was Jess' turn to snort. "Innocent? I've been around construction crews too long to lay claim to that title."

"Is that so?" The words slid off Devin's tongue, innuendo intended. The deep blush gracing Jess' cheeks brought out the devil in him. Being playful with a woman was new and surprisingly exciting. "Do tell."

"What I meant is that I heard a lot of things... not that I did..." Jess ducked her head. "Oh god, I'm making this worse."

Serenity burst out laughing, and Jess gave her the evil eye. "Don't you have some plants to get in the ground?"

Jess grabbed Devin by the arm and dragged him toward the back door. "And you, let's get that cabinet situation squared away."

"I love it when you get all domineering," he teased. She swatted his arm and chuckled. The sound hit him in the chest and somersaulted in his gut.

Jess waggled her eyebrows. "You ain't seen nothing yet. I've got handcuffs and a whip at home. I think we should try them out." She did a cocky little shoulder shimmy.

Devin staggered back with a hand to his chest. "Why Miss Winters, I had no idea." He leaned down and whispered in her ear. "But I'd sure like to explore your offer."

The color zoomed past her cheeks and suffused her entire face. "You do know I'm kidding? Right?"

Sighing dramatically, Devin stuck out his lower lip in a pout. "A man can dream." Sparing with her make him feel like the young adult he'd never had a chance to be, but he needed to give her a break. He nudged her with his elbow. "Of course, I know you're kidding. I like you the way you are. No game-playing required to get my attention."

She swiped her brow with the back of her hand and blew out a breath. "You had me going there."

He paused and touched her arm so she would face him. "Law's going to be in town Saturday morning to look at some property, and I'm going to meet him for about an hour. The rest of my day is free. It's supposed to be a nice weekend. Why don't we take my boat up to Folsom Lake and spend the day there?"

"I'd like that. I can even pack us a picnic lunch."

"I thought you didn't do kitchen stuff."

She looked at him like he'd sprouted a sign that read, '*world's dumbest man*'. He cringed. She might be right. "I'm sorry. I'm sure you're perfectly capable of putting together a picnic lunch. My bad. I mean all you need is cheese and crackers and maybe some fruit. Nothing fancy."

"You might want to stop talking. I don't think you can get any more of your foot in your mouth." Jess pinched her lips together but he could see the twinkle in her eyes.

"Right. Boot leather tastes terrible."

She chuckled and rolled her eyes. "You might not be familiar with the concept but they have these things in grocery stores called *deli departments*." She said the last two words slowly. "It's amazing what delicacies you can find there." She grinned as her voice trailed off and she started walking again. "There is every chance I might even be able to tempt your refined taste buds."

He patted his chest. "Be still my heart." His voice lowered and his tone grew serious. "You always tempt me." He opened the door and she ducked under his arm. Every pheromone in his body was on high alert as he called out, "Hey guys. Boss lady's here. Look busy."

# Chapter
# Fourteen

"WHAT DO YOU THINK?" Law asked.

Devin glanced up and down the street. Stepping forward, he cupped his hands against the window to block the glare and peered inside. He looked at his friend and shrugged. "It's an empty storefront. But then again, I'm hardly the one to judge prime real estate."

"But the location's not bad. You live here, so you should have a sense for that. Come on, walk with me."

Devin exhaled slowly and shook his head. Law's restless energy meant he seldom stood still. Constant motion. His hands flowed with his words, arching and diving and swirling.

"Yeah, downtown sees a lot of nightlife." Devin unzipped his hoody and let it hang open. The chill was off the morning and he looked forward to a mild day. "What did Ivy have to say? Does she think it's a good location?"

"She says these are worth considering for my new night club. I'm meeting her in an hour so she can show me the insides of these places, plus go over the specs she sent me." Law paused in front of another building, this one occupied by a run-down, mom and pop grocery store. He poked his head in the door and eyed the interior. "The purchase price in this area is lower because it's just outside the new basketball arena and event center renewal zone." He started walking again and Devin hurried to catch up. "Ivy doesn't expect that to last as more upscale businesses move in. Lots of potential for a good return on investment."

Law halted abruptly and Devin almost ran into him. "Hey pal, you need to signal lane changes," Devin groused.

"Sorry." Law rubbed his fashionably stubbled jaw. "What do you think about Ivy?"

Confusion furrowed Devin's brows. "Again, lane changes." He clapped a hand onto Law's shoulder. "Sometimes your lightning fast mind is hard for us lower IQ people to keep up with." He suspected there was more to his friend's question and wasn't above razzing him. Making a show of thinking, he took his time answering.

Law started walking again and Devin fell into step beside him. "I don't see Ivy as much as the other partners. She's mostly involved with the projects before and after construction. From what I've seen she's pretty no-nonsense. Driven. Could probably talk a grizzly out of the fish it just caught." Devin glanced sideways at his friend. "Why?"

"No reason. Just wondered."

Devin heard the shift in Law's voice. The casualness too forced. "*You like her.*"

"God, we sound like we're twelve." Law's nervous chuckle gave him away. "Maybe." He ran a hand over his hair. "Do you think she's seeing anyone?"

"Now we do sound like we're twelve and passing notes in math class." Devin followed Law inside a Starbucks. "I've heard she's dating some hot-shot lawyer, but I gather it's more convenient than serious."

They placed their orders and claimed one of the vacant tables. Law's gaze swept the space and Devin could almost see the charts and graphs spinning in his head. Law could calculate projected foot traffic, revenue per hour, and staffing needs with the speed of neurons firing.

"Probably much busier during the work week," Devin observed. "If you're interested in Ivy, I don't see any impediments. Go for it."

Law slid out of his seat and collected their orders.

When he sat back down, Devin's curiosity got the better of him. "It's not like you to hold back just because there might be another guy in the picture. What gives?"

"Maybe I'm not as pushy as I once was. Maybe I've mellowed." He took a quick sip of his coffee and almost spit it out. "Jesus, that's hot."

The light bulb went off in Devin's head. "You're nervous about Ivy." He stopped short of chortling with glee. "You've never dated a fellow tiger before, and you're not so sure of yourself." Devin slapped the table with his palm. "I love it."

"Oh shut up." Law scowled at him. "How's your investigation going? Turn up any juicy tidbits on your dad?"

Devin wasn't so easily deterred. "Ivy's a class act. While she might be too hot for you to handle, ask her out. She could take pity on you."

Another withering look took aim at Devin. "There's not a woman on the planet I can't charm."

A lesser man might have crumbled but Devin snorted. It wasn't often he saw his friend flustered. "Then what are you waiting for? I'll expect a status update tomorrow." Thinking about how his search for proof was going, ended the light-heartedness. His shoulders slumped. "The search? So far I've turned up zilch. Either my dad's not the villain I pegged him for, or he's bullied or bought off anyone who had a beef against him."

"My experience with your dad leads me to believe your instincts are spot on." Law ping-ponged his phone on the table back and forth between his hands. "Your dad's smart. He probably wrote the book on flying below the radar."

"If I can't find anything in the public records—and I've checked for mechanic liens and lawsuits—how am I going to prove anything?" Devin felt a twitch along his jaw. Before he'd moved back to Sacramento, he'd thought it would be easy to find proof. After so many years, surely someone would have filed a complaint and stood up to his dad. "I wish I knew more about business so I could spot things that don't add up."

Devin leaned forward resting his arms on the table. "Jess mentioned several contractors who threatened to file lawsuits, but obviously no one followed through. I've thought about reaching out to them, maybe pretending to be a reporter working on a story, to see if they'll talk to me. Thoughts?" He pressed a finger to his temple where a dull ache had taken hold.

Law sat back and fiddled with his phone for a few seconds then looked up. "That might work, but I suspect they wouldn't be straight with you. Getting taken is not something most business owners want to admit to. Any chance your brother might get on board? Do some digging?"

"Let's just say he's skeptical. Phil swears he's never seen anything out of line... most likely because dad has gotten better at covering his tracks. But then again, Phil's never had a reason to look too closely. He looks up to Dad the way Madison and I once did."

A far-away look took over Law's features. "How is Madi?"

"Great actually. Loves her job. Loves living back East." Devin bumped his friend's hand across the table. "She'll be out here on a visit in a few weeks. Wants to see how I'm settling in."

"That's so? We'll have to do something together. It'll be fun to see her again."

"You don't still have a thing for her, do you?"

The corner of Law's lips twitched up and his face relaxed. "No, but you never forget your first love."

"Good to hear, because she's seeing someone, and she hinted it might be serious." Devin watched his friend to gauge his reaction. The pressure eased on his chest when Law's smile looked genuine.

"Good for her. She deserves to be happy." Law glanced at the Rolex watch on his wrist. "Before I have to go, let's circle back to your problem. Any other ideas?"

"Just one. Do you think it would do any good to talk to Dad's old Chief Financial Officer, Ellen Bitterman? Her son, Steve, and I used to be friends so even though we lost touch, I think she'd see me."

"If anyone knows where the bodies are buried, my money's on Ellen. Wasn't she with your dad for a long time?"

"Twenty-five years. I heard she took early retirement a few years back. Had something to do with Steve's health. Though I also heard there was some friction with her leaving the firm." Hope fluttered deep in Devin's chest. Could this be the opening he needed? "Thanks for your perspective."

"Any time." Law stood. "I gotta go."

Devin walked with him out the door. The two exchanged a back-slap bro hug. As they went their separate ways, Devin waved his hand in the air and called over his shoulder, "Ask Ivy out, you big chicken." He laughed at the "*bawk, bawk*" sound from Law.

---

DEVIN HAD PICKED Jess up around ten and they'd driven to the lake. It felt good to hit the road with the windows down, music station blaring out hits from the nineties, and a few puffy white clouds dotting a crystalline blue sky. They'd put the pontoon boat in the water around eleven, cruised the lake in a meandering fashion, soaking in the sun until they got hungry, and finally beached their craft on a secluded, sandy beach. Devin decided this must be what people called carefree. Not that he had much experience with that lifestyle, but he had dreamed life could be this way.

"Any particular reason for the shit-eating grin on your face?" Jess offered Devin a plate and set the container of fried chicken and a pile of napkins between them on the blanket.

"Other than life is good, I don't have a reason." And right this moment, life was good. The water lapped lightly against the rocks along the shore. He took a bite of chicken and let his gaze wander. Under the shade of a large oak, its leaves rustling softly in the slight breeze, contentment suffused his body. Jess scooted over to sit beside him, her bare knee grazing his. His skin tingled where they touched. Her hair smelled faintly of roses. Eventually he'd have to tell her why he'd returned to town and prayed he wouldn't lose her.

Jess' face softened as she looked sideways at him under her lashes. "That's a pretty good reason to smile." She spooned a healthy amount of potato salad onto her plate and selected a drumstick from the bucket. "These strawberries were too beautiful to resist."

She plucked one from the basket and took a bite. Devin captured the bit of juice that trickled to her chin with his finger. He stuck that finger in his mouth and sucked.

Jess cleared her throat, and he watched the blush tinge her cheeks. "I'm going to leave the salads and fruit in the cooler to keep the bugs out."

"As long as you're not trying to keep me out, we're good." He leaned over to peruse the contents of the cooler. "I've seen the potato salad and strawberries. What else have you got in there?" He cracked the lid on another container. "Coleslaw, always a good choice." He opened a flat box. "What's this?"

"Roasted vegetables... red peppers, zucchini, and asparagus... drizzled with a garlic-infused olive oil." She chuckled. "I sound like a commercial but it looked good... and healthy. If we like it, we could try making some on the grill next summer. It doesn't look too hard."

"Next summer. I like the sound of that." He couldn't keep the smile off his face. "Any chance the real reason you went for the vegetables was that you were feeling a little guilty about loading up on the comfort food?"

She rolled her eyes. "Okay, you caught me. We are adults, after all, and should set a good example."

"Who says?" He pushed a strand of hair behind her ear, just because his fingers itched to touch her.

"I'm sure it's in the adulting manual." She nibbled on a slice of zucchini and her eyes widened then closed.

Her hum of pleasure seeped down his throat like fresh squeezed lemonade, tangy and attention-getting.

"I'm glad I bought these," she said. "Tasty."

Devin leaned in and pressed his lips to hers. His tongue traced her lips and he enjoyed the hint of garlic he found there. "You're right. Tasty."

Easing back he gave her some space. Together they watched a Kingfisher dive for the water and fly away with some morsel in its beak. A pair of squirrels edged ever closer hoping for a handout.

"What made you decide to be a contractor? It's not exactly at the top of every little girl's wish list." Devin helped himself to some coleslaw and watched her ponder his question. He loved the way her nose wrinkled when she concentrated.

"Short answer? From the time I was little, I gravitated toward blocks and Legos. Much to the disappointment of my mom, dolls got left on the shelf. I enjoyed building things. Seeing a vision in my head become a physical thing—that was my passion. As I got older…" Jess sighed. "I found myself crafting places that felt like home—or what home should be. A place where people feel loved, respected, and comfortable being who they are. That's what I'm trying to create with each project I tackle."

"Tall order." Devin cupped her face between his palms. His thumbs lightly stroked her cheeks. He hated that her childhood, like his, had punched holes in their self-esteem. He wanted her to believe how much she meant to him. She hadn't brought up what they'd said to each other the night her dad went into the hospital, and for now it was best to let it rest. He had a mission to accomplish and had better get on with it. "I gather you dad doesn't share your philosophy?"

Jess snorted. "That would be a no." She chewed on her bottom lip. "I'd like to think it was simply a different era, more cutthroat and one where profit came before any other consideration. But it's more than that. Dad's a very competitive person with a boatload of pride. If he isn't first, then he's nothing."

Devin lowered his lips to hers for a brief kiss, wishing he could wave a wand and make things right between Jess and her dad. "Do you think that's how his business got in trouble? He was too competitive and got in over his head?"

Her chin rested on her chest as she inhaled slowly. "I do." Her fingers slowly swept across his forehead smoothing his worry lines. "He hates feeling like he's come up short. I think that's why he resents my success because it makes him feel less. Does that make sense?"

"Sort of. Still hard for me to wrap my brain around. When I have kids, I hope I'm their biggest fan and always ready to cheer them on." The thought of Jess, her belly round with their child popped into his head, and his breath stilled.

"I can picture you as that kind of dad. Rooting for your kids to reach for the stars." Her hand dropped to his knee and the warmth of her touch made his heart beat faster. "Dad moved up in the industry the old fashioned way. Started on a crew. Worked up to crew foreman and finally branched out on his own as a general contractor. In his mind that's the way it should be done. When I got my degree in Construction Management, I think he saw that as somehow short-circuiting the process."

"You said you thought it was a bad business deal that ruined his business. Do you think that pride kept him from going after the guy he was dealing with?"

"Probably."

"Do you think he'll ever go after him?"

"Doubt he'd ever want the news to get out. He'd be too embarrassed." Jess shrugged.

"What if he wasn't at fault? What if he were cheated and lost money because of that? Do you think he'd want to make the guy pay for what he'd done?" God he hoped so. If her dad was willing to come forward, Devin could finally tell her the truth about himself.

"That's an interesting theory. What makes you think that?"

A light sweat broke out on Devin's forehead. "Something you'd said about this TLM Investments cheating other contractors. Made me wonder if your dad was one of them." He shrugged, hoping she bought his casual interest act.

Her brows creased as she assessed him. "I don't know if he'd go after him, but given my dad's state of mind, I'm not sure that would be a healthy approach for him. I'm afraid he'd be in it for revenge instead of bringing the guy to justice."

"Fair enough. It's just a shame the guy has probably been getting away with this kind of thing for years."

"Enough of this. Tell me something about yourself. What did you want to be when you grew up—other than a hellion?"

"My past isn't pretty, so I'll admit that it's like picking at a scab to rehash it." He traced an infinity symbol in the dirt and kept his eyes downcast as he spoke. "But it's only fair to let you know the mess that you've gotten yourself in to by getting involved with me." He rubbed his damp hands on his shorts. All the old disappointment and shame he felt at who he'd been slammed against him.

She touched his arm with one hand and with a finger under his chin, urged him to look at her. "I don't see it that way. I sense a strength and compassion in you that could only come from what you've been through. Never discount how experience has molded you."

Hope took up residence and lifted the heavy weight that sat on his soul. Could he be that young child he once stared at in the mirror? The one who couldn't wait to grow up and be like his dad—a man he thought could walk on water? Respected and honorable? With Jess by his side, he knew he could be that man—not his father's man but his own man.

"For a brief time, I wanted to be a cowboy, but for most of my young life, I wanted to be like my dad, a businessman. Can't say I really knew what that meant, but people seemed to look up to him. People listened to what he had to say. Seemed like I could do a lot worse than being just like him."

"What happened to change your opinion?"

Devin couldn't go there yet. "Turns out he wasn't the paragon of virtue I thought he was." The weight was back and his lungs didn't expand and contract the way they should. Her hand rubbed circles on his back and his lungs remembered what they were supposed to do.

"Yeah, the day Santa falls off his sleigh is hard on the psyche," she said.

A chuckle rumbled through his chest. "You got that right. I suppose all parents lose their luster at some point. Mine just happened to topple from the Empire State Building." He put an arm around her shoulder and pulled her close. "Anyway, I'm still trying to figure out what I want to be. Do you think I'm too old to be considered for the astronauts program?"

She swatted his arm. "Naw, I'm pretty sure they have geriatric equipment up there." Her face turned serious. "Does being back home bring back a lot of bad memories?"

"Bad and good, I suppose. I did have a lot of fun growing up. It wasn't all doom and gloom. I had friends at school and did the usual boy stuff—baseball, scouting, and goofing off." With his arm hooked around her neck, he pulled her in and kissed the top of her head.

"I guess that's typical. No one has it all good. There's always something that dims the light," Jess sighed.

He shook the empty bag that had contained the cookies. "What do you say we walk off some of this food and then get back in the water? I hear the sunset from the lake is a must see."

Later, as they reclined on the floor of the boat, wrapped in each other's arms and watched the sun set behind the hills in a burst of color, he vowed he would do whatever it took to keep her in his life. Even if that meant he ultimately had to give up his quest for justice. He just hoped he could live with himself if that were the case.

# Chapter Fifteen

AWKWARD. DEVIN HADN'T SEEN Ellen Bitterman in almost twenty years, so it was just like meeting her for the first time. The impulse to remain quiet and reserved hit hard. Until people got to know him and, more importantly, he trusted them enough to open up, everyone assumed he was withdrawn. He needed her to respond to him. That meant pasting on a smile and delivering the small talk he'd practiced.

After knocking on the door, he tried to figure out what to do with his hands and settled for clasping his hands in front of him. He'd taken care with his attire, dressing in cotton slacks, a casual, long-sleeved dress shirt, and brown leather shoes. The images he'd seen on the web made men wearing outfits like this seem open and friendly.

Ellen opened the door and smiled at him. The curve of her lips was the one he remembered, glad to see him—but the rest of her had changed dramatically. Where she had once been pleasantly plump, she now was gaunt. Her once thick, dark hair which she'd kept in a meticulous bun at the back of her head, was now completely silver and hung loosely past her shoulders. Instead of a business suit, she wore loose-fitting jeans and a cotton top that swallowed her thin frame.

Devin broadened his smile, doing his best to hide his shock. "Hello Mrs. Bitterman. Thank you for seeing me. I know it's been a long time."

"Too long, and please call me Ellen. You're a grown man now. No sense standing on formalities." She took his arm in a surprisingly strong grip and motioned him inside with her head. "I'm glad for the company. My Sundays can be lonely."

She led him into a modestly furnished living room situated just off the entry. He sat on the overstuffed, floral-print sofa she indicated.

"Would you like some iced tea?" Ellen asked.

"That would be nice." He watched her walk out of the room then let his gaze wander. A dark brown recliner sat opposite the sofa with a wooden coffee table in between. A small rectangular end table nestled beside the chair with a paperback mystery novel resting there. A stained-glass lamp hung from a chain overhead. The heavy drapes were open to let in the light from the large picture window. A credenza sat along one wall covered in framed photos.

He got up to examine them and was holding one of him and Steve, fishing poles in hand, when Ellen reentered the room. She placed the tray she carried on the coffee table. He put the photo down and resumed his place on the sofa. So many memories. The images of Steve going to prom, in his high school baseball uniform, graduating from college—they reminded him of all he had missed and how much of his youth he had wasted in anger and bitterness.

"I thought you might like some cookies," She held a plate out to him along with a paper napkin. She set a coaster on the coffee table and a glass of tea on it before easing into the recliner.

"That's real nice." He took a bite. "Chocolate chip. You always made the best. So, how is retirement treating you? Getting to do all the things you always put off when you were working?"

He watched her face fall and dread stabbed him in the gut cold as an icicle. "I'm sorry, did I say something wrong?"

"No, you're fine. Retirement just didn't turn out like I expected." She dabbed at her eye with her napkin. "I guess you haven't heard. Steve passed away."

"Oh my God. I'm so sorry. I know how close you two were. What happened? I heard you retired early because Steve had some health problems, but I had no idea it was so serious."

"Leukemia. The doctors tried everything they could, but he didn't respond to any of the treatments." She dabbed at her eyes again and blew her nose.

Devin went to her, and drew her into his arms hugging her and rocking her as she sobbed. Her tears wet his shirt and his heart cracked a little wider. He was glad he'd come, but he couldn't ask her the questions he'd come to ask. She'd been through so much and sure didn't need him prying into the past—a past she might not be proud of if she'd had any part in covering up his dad's dishonesty.

She finally drew away after filling her lungs with a deep breath and sat back down.

"When did he pass away?" Devin asked.

Ellen brought the glass of tea to her lips and sipped. "Just over a year ago."

"Steve never married?" Devin hoped she had some grandchildren to ease the hole in her heart.

"He'd just gotten engaged when he was diagnosed. They decided to put off the wedding until he was better." Devin watched her swallow. "Shannon, that's his fiancée's name, stayed by his side till the end. She stops by sometimes to check on me, but she's young and will eventually move on with her life."

"Again, I'm so sorry. I can't imagine your life without him." He cast about for something to say. Something that didn't sound inane. He had no idea how to comfort her, then remembered a snippet from one of his therapy sessions. Talk about the good memories. "In one of the photos, I saw Steve at what I'm guessing was his college graduation. You must have been so proud."

"He went to UC Davis and studied Veterinary Science. Loved animals and wanted to take care of them. His life was just coming together when it exploded." Ellen dabbed at her eyes again.

"What are you going to do now? Do you plan to stay in the area?"

"This is my home. I grew up here. My sister still lives nearby and my brother is in San Jose so not too far away. I'm adjusting." She sipped her tea. "I recently started volunteering at the local animal shelter... the same one Steve volunteered at. Being around the animals that need love helps and I think Steve would've approved. Makes me feel like I'm honoring his memory."

"I think you're right. Steve would approve." A tabby cat strolled into the room, tail in the air, and hopped on Ellen's lap. "Looks like you brought your work home with you."

She ran her hand over the cat's back. "You were always a good boy. I was sad when your parents sent you away. I had a feeling nothing good would come of that." She looked at him, her expression questioning.

"You went from sweet to wild in such a short time. I assume it wasn't the typical teenage brain malfunction?"

There was his opening but did he want to take it? Devin rubbed his sweaty palms on his slacks. Yes, he did. Ellen would either share what she knew or not. He wouldn't press.

"When I was about fourteen, I learned something about Dad and his business practices that changed how I looked at him." His heart thumped in his chest and his stomach felt like he was on the downward dip of a rollercoaster. "He cheated people out of money he owed them and didn't care that his actions ruined peoples' lives." There. He'd said it.

"Ah, I see." Ellen nodded slowly as she spoke.

Devin couldn't read her expression and held his breath.

After what seemed like an eternity, Ellen spoke her tone low and tinged with sadness. "You're right. Your dad's as crooked as a sidewinder slithering across the desert. Refusing to pay people what he owed them is just the tip of the iceberg. As it's known in popular terms, his more serious crime involved cooking the books."

She continued to stroke the cat in her lap, its purr the only sound until Devin recovered from the bombshell and could speak again. It felt like the walls were closing in on him. Sweat popped out on his forehead. What he'd suspected all these years was not only true but so much worse. He only wished he felt better about it. "You knew then? And what do you mean cooking the books?" Turns out he wasn't the only one who'd kept the secret and could have stopped his father.

"Not right away. In fact it was years before I began uncovering documents that made me wonder if something wasn't quite right.

Invoices and disbursements that didn't make sense. Expenses charged to the company that seemed off."

The cat hopped off her lap, possibly sensing the tension in the room, and walked away, its tail twitching. Ellen's face took on a pinched looked, but she stared straight into Devin's eyes. Never wavered. He detected resolve in the set to her shoulders.

"Your dad knew how to cover his tracks, I'll give him that." Ellen cleared her throat. "I may have been the CFO, but it turns out there was a lot I didn't have access to."

"How is that possible?" Devin asked.

"When I was hired, it was the firm's policy to have data entry clerks enter the totals from all the payables and receivables into a bookkeeping program. These clerks didn't have the expertise to look at the numbers and assess whether or not everything looked legit. They simply typed in the figures in front of them. I never saw the original paperwork, only the financial reports generated from the data. Unless something looked way out of whack, I had no reason to dig any deeper." Ellen sat on the edge of the recliner, feet together, and hands tightly clasped in her lap.

"So what finally tipped you off?"

She sat up straight, one elbow resting on the arm hugging her waist and a finger crooked across her mouth. A mirthless chuckle finally escaped. "A routine audit had me go back and check some historical records. I noticed that past expenditures for things like cleaning supplies, appliances, carpet, paint... the kinds of purchases one would expect to maintain residential rental units... used to be purchased from small suppliers. The year before I was hired, I noticed that all purchases started coming from just one company—Consolidated Building Supplies. If it had been a less expensive way to acquire the supplies, it would have made sense."

"But that wasn't the case?"

"No, it wasn't. I went back and compared the costs on old invoices to the current ones and noticed that prices ran about twenty to twenty-five percent higher from Consolidated. When I mentioned this to your dad, he told me my job was to make sure all the financial statements were in order and let him run the business."

"Why do I get the feeling there's more to this story?"

"It took years to put all the puzzle pieces together but do you know who owns Consolidated Business Supplies?"

"No." Devin had a sinking feeling that he wasn't going to like the answer.

"You, your sister, and your brother. Your dad set up that company, along with a few others, when you were about nine and made himself the trustee. He expensed the inflated Consolidated invoices against TLM Investments so it was a business write-off for him and then pocketed the difference between the actual costs to purchase the supplies and what he charged himself on the invoices. Technically, the money he pocketed belonged to you kids but I'm betting you never heard anything about it."

"Are you serious? How could he do that? How could we own companies and not know about them?" Devin felt like he'd just gone ten rounds with the heavyweight champ. This was so much bigger than he'd imagined. He felt lightheaded. His father hadn't just cheated people he'd done business with. Ellen had laid out a scenario where he was using his own children to shield whatever he was up to from public scrutiny.

"You were young when he created these companies. After you reached majority and he had to dissolve the trusts, my guess is he forged signatures for each of you on the various companies' incorporation documents and bank records. I can't be sure, since he used several outside accountants and attorneys to manage these companies. I did get some bank statements sent to TLM Investments once—I assume that was in error because I never saw any others—for the companies in your name which is how I first learned they existed."

"So he gets extra revenue from these companies that me, Madison, and Philip own, why hide it? Didn't he, or we, have to pay taxes on the income?" Devin scratched his head. None of this made sense. He didn't understand how his dad benefited from this deception.

"If I had to guess, now that you're all adults and paying taxes on your own incomes, he filed the corporate taxes on your behalf but used a phony business address for all correspondence, so you'd never know. Over the years, I found hints in TLM Investment records that he has shell companies and off-shore accounts where your revenue goes. It might all be perfectly legal, but if he's hiding things, then I suspect not." She leaned across the coffee table and touched his arm. "I did a little digging in public records and found deeds to multiple properties in each of your names." She sighed.

"How could I have missed this in my records search?" Devin scratched his head.

"You would had to have known what companies to search for. The properties were bought by the corporations and not by specific individuals."

Ellen spent the next hour outlining tax evasion schemes where his dad had provided deflated property value information to the IRS, bank fraud where he inflated the value of those same properties to get loans, how he'd run personal expenses—like home remodeling projects and trips—through as business expenses, and what she'd heard about his dealings with contractors who worked on his properties. She described the potential for money laundering. There was more even she probably didn't know about. As Devin had overheard so many years ago his dad lied, cheated, and bullied anyone who worked for him. By the time she finished, Devin was emotionally drained.

"If you knew all of this, why didn't you go to the authorities?" There had to be a good reason. Ellen was an ethical person and he'd be surprised if she'd turned a blind eye.

She closed her eyes and circled her fingers on her temples. When she looked at him again, he could see the pain in her eyes.

"Lots of reasons. If the company collapsed, a lot of good people who counted on the paychecks from your dad would suffer. By the time I figured out the scheme your dad had involved you kids in—you and Madison were over eighteen—and I wasn't sure what kind of legal jeopardy you might be liable for. This kind of tax fraud isn't my area of expertise and without your dad's permission I couldn't legally talk to another accounting professional. I didn't want to approach anyone in law enforcement until I knew for sure what was illegal and what was merely unethical."

She rubbed a hand over her face. "Finally, when I had a better sense of the scope of what he was doing, he got wind of how I'd been poking around and he and gave me an ultimatum. Steve had just gotten sick. Your dad said if I left quietly and kept what I knew to myself, he'd put Steve on the payroll so he'd qualify for medical insurance and keep me on the payroll as a consultant." She looked down. "I'm not proud that I took the deal but Steve needed the insurance and I needed the income."

Devin put a hand on her shoulder. "I understand. You had to protect Steve. Seems like I'm back to square one. No proof."

"That's not entirely true." She stood. "Wait here."

When she returned, she handed him a USB drive. "I made copies of everything I found over the years plus blind-copied to my home computer all emails that might be relevant to uncovering what your dad has done."

A sudden thought punched him in the gut. "Do you think Phil is in on any of this?" His dad going to jail was one thing, but his brother... that was too much.

"No, I'm convinced he's in the dark as much as you were. Everything I know about Phil's dealings are on the up and up."

"Now what do I do? I don't want to get you into legal trouble." Could this whole mess get any more tangled? Could Devin be in legal trouble for owning companies and properties he knew nothing about? He had a lot to learn before he brought any of this to the light of day.

"I'm pretty sure I could become a cooperating witness and avoid most jeopardy. I might face some punishment for staying quiet, but I'm ready to accept whatever the courts decide." She brushed a lock of his hair back from his forehead like she'd done when Devin was a child. "What you do with the information I've given you is up to you. You might also want to see what you can find out about the companies your dad set up in your name." She cocked her head and looked at him curiously. "If you don't mind my asking, why are you so intent on getting all this out in the open?"

"Guilt, I suppose. I knew and didn't even try to go to the authorities. I took the cowards way out, afraid that no one would believe a kid in high school. People were hurt because I said nothing." He rubbed his hands on his thighs feeling comforted by the motion. "In some way I feel responsible for the people my dad harmed. I'd like to bring justice to them if I can." He held up the USB drive. "Hopefully what I need to do that is in here."

Ellen reached over and took both his hands in hers, looking him directly in the eye. "You didn't know about all of this. The only thing you knew was that your dad refused to pay people what he owed them." She squeezed his hands. "Did that hurt them? Yes, but even if you'd gone to the authorities, without the companies that had suffered a loss filing a complaint, it would only have been hearsay. You need to let go of that guilt you've been carting around."

Devin stood feeling a little better. Ellen was right. There was little he could have done. "I should be going." He folded her in a tight hug. "I'll be in touch about my plans. I promise I won't be a stranger."

As he climbed into his truck, a heavy weight pressed on his shoulders. What he had once thought was so straightforward, put more kinks than his neck than sleeping on the ground. So many ramifications. Ellen. Possibly himself and Madison. Phil. The people who worked for his dad. The only bright spot was that he could tell Jess who he was and what his dad had done to her dad. With all this new information, he didn't need to open those old wounds unless the people his dad had cheated wanted to file complaints. With a sigh, he turned the key in the ignition and pulled away from the curb. He had a lot to think about.

# Chapter Sixteen

WHAT A DOWNER. Sunday dinner with her family. Compared to yesterday on the lake with Devin and last night in his arms… Jess might as well be sitting in detention for something someone else had done.

Jess, her sister, and brother-in-law sat wedged together on the sofa. Miserable and uncomfortable. Their dad stretched out on his recliner shouting insults at the television and the poor performance of the football team he wanted to win. Their mom sat beside her husband in a straight-backed chair from the dining room and held his hand—at least when said hand wasn't fisted and shaking at the referees.

Dressed in jeans, cotton t-shirts, and flip flops—no makeup and their hair pulled into low ponytails—Jess and Hannah were in stark contrast to their mom. As usual, Darlene was turned out in freshly-pressed knit slacks, a stylish silky top, sparkly sandals, makeup and hair like she'd just stepped out of the beauty shop. Jess figured her dad must have done something right to have their mom still working hard to impress him after all these years.

Bob leaned around Hannah. "Saw the renderings for your new building yesterday."

Jess' stomach clenched and she put a finger to her lips. "The weather's so nice. You guys want to take our wine outside?" She jerked her head to the side indicating they should follow her lead. "Don't want to disturb Dad's game."

"Nothing to disturb. These guys are playing like crap." Her dad's scowl deepened, a feat Jess didn't think possible. "You sneaking off to talk about me behind my back?"

The sigh in Jess' soul swept her up in a dark cloud of frustration and resignation. Maybe her dad was incapable of change. This is who he is and the sooner she accepted it, the better for her mental health. "No dad, we just want to enjoy the sunshine and catch up without bothering you."

Darlene patted her husband's hand. "Now dear, no one's talking about you." She planted a quick kiss on his cheek. "Except maybe to say good things. Leave them be."

A rueful smile tugged at the corner of Jess' mouth. Mom the peacemaker. But the way her dad's face softened when he looked at his wife gave her pause. Despite his crusty disposition with everyone else, her dad could love someone.

Gerry's devilish grin turned him into a different person. "If they go out in the yard, that means I get you to myself for a while."

Jess looked heavenward as a blush crept into her mother's cheeks. It made her happy though to see this lighter side to her dad. "Okay you two, we can take a hint." Scooting to the edge of the sofa, she picked up her wine and made her way to the backyard.

"Thanks for the excuse to escape," Hannah said once they were all seated around the small teak table under the new gazebo. "I must admit, Serenity is a miracle worker. This landscaping redesign makes it actually pleasant to be out here now. I'm glad we talked them into fixing the yard up. Do you think mom and dad get some use out of it now?"

"Mom says they do," Jess said. "Dad's even consented to using the grill we bought him. I'm amazed he agreed to spend the money on something as frivolous as fixing up the backyard." She lowered her voice to mimic their dad. "*No one's going to see it but us. What's the point?*"

"Wonders will never cease. Maybe mom's beginning to rub off on him." Hannah giggled. "Did you know mom even roped me into going with her to the nursery to pick out a few pots and flowers? They look nice around the edge of the gazebo."

Jess leaned sideways, peering over the railing to examine her mom's foray into gardening. "I hadn't noticed. That is a nice touch. Love the pretty yellow and blue pots you picked out." She shifted to face Bob. "I'm sorry I shushed you, but any mention of our new office building and Dad's blood pressure shoots through the roof."

"No problem. As soon as the words were out of my mouth, I remembered how he reacted when you brought it up before." He stretched his long, lanky legs out in front of him and brushed his thinning hair to the side. "This is the life. Birds singing. Warm fall day. Out from under your dad's evil eye." He reached over and squeezed Hannah's hand. "No offense."

"No offense taken. Dad's easier to take in small doses," Hannah said. "So tell us about the plans for your office building. Bob couldn't stop raving about them."

"How did you end up seeing them?" Jess asked. "Checking in with your architect on the renderings for your new house?" She hid her grin behind her wine glass. Hannah and Bob's excitement was contagious.

"Guilty as charged." Bob ducked his head but couldn't conceal his pleasure.

"We'll be able to pour the foundation as soon as you pull the permits, Mr. Planning Department Guy." Jess poked him in the ribs with her elbow. "I'd like to get the foundation in place and cured while the weather holds."

"Out of my hands." Bob raised his hands. "Our lot is in a different planning department jurisdiction, but they did promise they'd put a rush on the review as a courtesy to a fellow professional." Bob grinned at his wife. "We'd like to be in by next spring so we can move forward with starting our family."

Jess watched her sister blush and felt a tender glow. "I'll do my best to keep everything on track. Hopefully we won't have a super rainy winter." Her feet did a jig against the wood deck. "As far as our new offices, I'm beyond thrilled."

"I liked the modified Victorian-style elevation. Really classy," Bob said.

"Thanks. We thought that wouldn't overpower the neighborhood but still stand out. Two stories gives us space for us and two or three tenants."

"That's smart. Tenants will help defray costs," Hannah said.

"We thought so too. A sandwich shop owner has already expressed interest."

"You haven't even broken ground yet. How'd they hear about the project?" Hannah asked.

"We eat there a lot and they overheard us talking about it." Jess shrugged but her insides were shooting off fireworks. "The lot's big enough so we'll have plenty of parking, and that's a draw for many neighborhood businesses. We also have enough space to build a storage building in the back where Victoria can store her furniture inventory and Serenity can store her landscaping supplies. That allows us to eliminate our storage expense. Serenity's bummed we can't have a greenhouse on the property but we're adding some skylights to a section of the storage building so she can start seedlings."

"So you're still going through with this cockamamie idea?" Jess jumped at the sound of her dad's gruff voice. None of them had seen him come out of the side yard by the garage and amble their direction.

Bob stood. "Come on Hannah. We should go check on your mom." He extended his hand to her. "Sounds like Jess and Gerry have some things to talk about."

From the look on Hannah's face, she appreciated the chance to move out of the line of fire. Jess turned her head so only Bob and Hannah could see and stuck out her tongue. Dipping into the well of resolve and strength she knew she possessed, Jess decided it was high time she had that long-overdue conversation with her dad.

"Yes, Uniquely Yours is moving forward with its plans." Jess swiped at some loose hair that had slipped out of her ponytail. "We've run the numbers, and it's a good business decision."

"In my day we didn't need all the glam and glitz you're going for." His face wrinkled in disgust but there was something else there as well. It took her a minute to put her finger on it. Envy. He always wanted to be the big man—the wheeler and dealer. He must see this move as one-upping him. Another example of Jess accomplishing what he'd never been able to.

"Like I said before, times have changed." She rested her hand on his arm. He flinched but didn't pull away. "A contractor's office is now a reflection of the quality of their work. If clients walk into a..." Oh lord, how could she put this tactfully? "... a place of business that isn't inviting and neat and orderly, then they jump to the conclusion that the work might be sub-par." She pinched the bridge of her nose.

"I get it. You need to be better than the competition." She heard the grudging respect in his voice. Her mouth dropped open and her head whipped around in a double take.

Jess sucked in a quick breath to quell her quaking stomach. "As a woman contractor, I have to be doubly conscious of the impression I make. Clients are predisposed to think that men will do a better job." She bit her bottom lip. "I can't just be good. I have to be excellent. I have to stand out. That's one of the reasons I formed Uniquely Yours. We give our customers something extra. We're the whole package."

He nodded. "Construction is a tough business. It's hard enough for a man to succeed. Women go into it with three strikes against them. Maybe that's why I always tried to discourage you." A small smile played about his lips and Jess almost fell off her chair. "I guess I should have known better, the way you always followed me around and dressed the dolls your mom gave you in overalls and hard hats."

"Is that a joke, Dad?" Jess choked out the words. "What's gotten in to you?"

"I guess." Red tinged his ears and he looked away. When he returned his gaze to his daughter, his face was somber. "Are you really sure TLM

149

Investment's lot is the only one that will suit? I don't trust that guy and would hate for you to get hurt."

Stunned. Had the bottom dropped out of her world? "You're worried about me? What's happened to you?"

"Maybe that hospital stay softened me up," he grumbled under his breath. "Course I'm worried about you. Aren't dads supposed to want to protect their children?" His tone turned sharp and accusatory.

"Yeah." She drew out the word, giving her brain time to recalibrate. She'd fallen down the rabbit hole of life and didn't know which door to choose. "I always thought you didn't want me to join your firm because I wasn't the son you wanted."

"I did want a son to follow in my footsteps. Like I said, I don't think this is a business for a woman. You gotta be tough to scrap and fight for every job. To do the physical labor the job requires. To face the danger of being on a job site. Stuff falling. People getting injured. A man's supposed to keep women safe. How could I do that if you went into business with me?" Jess saw the sadness in her father's eyes.

Dad, I don't need protection. I can take care of myself. What I've always wanted from you is respect. Respect that I'm doing a good job." It felt good to get that off her chest.

"I can see you're doing a good job. I hear the praise for your work." His scowl softened slightly.

"So you're okay with me being a general contractor?" Jess held her breath.

"No. Didn't say that. I'll always wish you'd chosen to be a librarian, or a secretary, or a housewife." His eyes brightened. "A housewife with a bunch of kids." He ran a hand over his balding head. "I don't like it, but I'm coming to accept that you're gonna do what you're gonna do."

"That sounds like a truce." Jess stuck out her hand and her dad shook it.

"Truce, but I still don't like you dealing with TLM Investments."

"We don't trust him either, but we've been looking for the right lot for over a year. This is the first one that we all could visualize as our permanent home. A place where we could design our office space to best serve our clients and really be part of the community instead of stuck in some business park." She touched her dad's arm again. "Don't worry. We've written so many contingencies into the contract that the man had better keep his checkbook handy. No phase moves forward until he's paid for the last phase and..." she tapped his arm with her finger. "We close escrow on the lot before we start any work on his remodel project. We meet with him tomorrow to finalize the plans. We'll only file for the permits once the land is in our names—free and clear."

"If you're sure. It does sound like you know what you're doing." He scowled at her. "Still not convinced you're not biting off more than you can chew, but if you need any help, I'll do what I can. I still know some people."

Jess chewed on her lip. Much as she hated to spoil this temporary truce with her dad, she had to ask. "What really happened with you and TLM Investments? It has to be more than a little business disagreement."

A muscle jumped along his jaw and his eyes narrowed. She was afraid he was going to brush her off, then he sighed. He looked across the yard and not at her as he spoke. "Thomas Miller came to me with a deal where I'd build a commercial building on a property he owned. Once the site was built out, he'd sell it, and we'd split the profits after he paid me back for the construction costs. I'd also have the exclusive contract to customize the space for each tenant." He licked his lips. "It looked like my chance to break into the big time."

Jess' gut clenched. "Let me guess, Thomas didn't hold up his end of the bargain?"

"He paid me for some of my construction costs when he sold the property but I was left holding the bag for most of the costs—and I didn't see a dime of the profit from the sale. What was I to do" He owned the land after all." He stared at Jess with an intensity that made her heart hurt for him.

"Why didn't you take him to court?"

"Because I was stupid. We had a contract, but it was mostly a handshake. That's how partners did business back then." He blew out a breath. "I didn't want people to know what an idiot I'd been. Besides, I didn't have the kind of cash it would have taken to fight him." He pointed a finger at her. "You can't say a word about this to anyone."

"I won't say a word. Promise. Thanks for letting me know what happened." Jess grinned. "Should we go back in and join the others? Let everyone know I have your blessing to be a general contractor?"

"I don't know about that, missy. That might be a bridge too far for this old guy. Accept that I'll help where I can but I'm not going to like it and still don't approve."

Jess walked beside her dad's as they strolled across the yard and for once wasn't suffering from a case of indigestion. Maybe her dad was mellowing.

# Chapter
# Seventeen

"I NEED YOUR SIGNATURE on all three copies on the pages with the *sign here* flags," Ivy instructed. "And your initials at the bottom of every page, both copies. Once everything is signed and the land is transferred to us, we can get started on our part of the deal—remodeling your home."

Thomas Miller's pen hovered over the first place requiring his signature.

The hint of a feral smile graced Ivy's lips. Jess bit her cheek to keep from grinning and waited. Thomas Miller may have the reputation as a shrewd negotiator but Jess had never seen anyone best Ivy.

"Do you have a question?" Cool. Calm. Controlled. That's their Ivy.

"I still have the option of making changes to the plans during construction, don't I? This doesn't lock me in to this exact plan, correct?" Thomas asked.

"Of course you do. We know that a client's vision might change during the course of the project." Ivy picked up the twenty page document and flipped to the appropriate page. "Right here." She tapped a page with her bright red manicured fingernail, "and I'm paraphrasing but you're welcome to reread it for yourself." She cleared her throat. "*Any changes to the original plan will trigger an addendum to the budget which must be approved and signed by the client and the contractor to acknowledge any subsequent increases or decreases said change will make to the budget. Once work on the new budget item has been completed, that budget item must be paid in full during the phase of the contract in which it was initiated before work can commence on the next phase of the project. The various phases and payment deadlines are all detailed in the original work schedule.*" Ivy's voice floated across the room smooth as silk.

"What if the work doesn't meet with my satisfaction? Don't I have the right to renegotiate the price in the contract?"

"Naturally, though all work halts on the project until the issue has been resolved through binding arbitration. Would you like a few more minutes to review the contract again?" Ivy smoothed a hand over her chin-length curly hair.

"No, I'm fine. Are all your contracts this tight?"

Ivy smiled sweetly, raised her brows, and shrugged. "We like to think we cover all our bases."

Thomas got busy affixing his signature to the document. To Jess it appeared that he pressed down with the pen harder than was necessary to get the job done. She turned her head to hide her grin. She couldn't care less that this particular client wasn't happy he had no wiggle room. Too bad. So sad.

After he set his pen down, Ivy leafed through the contract to make sure the paperwork was in order. "Everything looks good. Here's your copy. Now if you have the deposit check, I can take all of this to escrow and Jess will file for the building permits on your remodel."

He extended his hand and did that double-handed shake with each of the partners. A touch too intimate for Jess' taste but she supposed there must be people who responded positively to that approach. She glanced at her friends. But not in this group. They all wore polite expressions tinged with an underlying hint of '*I'd rather be holding a dead fish*'.

Judging solely on outward appearances Jess imagined Thomas turned lots of female heads. Tall—over six feet—he had the tan, chiseled features of a movie star. Blonde hair, stylishly mussed on top, close cropped on the sides and parted on the left. Clean-shaven and athletic. His tailored suit shouted designer. It was that below-the-surface creepiness that made Jess want to put a barrier between them.

"I look forward to working with you ladies." With that, he tugged on his cuffs, stepped outside on the portico, and trotted down the steps of the mansion they'd start work on next week.

Once he'd roared off in his Mercedes, Jess let out a sigh of relief and sagged against the wall. "Looks like we've officially stepped into the lion's den. I sure hope everyone has their battle armor ready."

"Don't you think it's odd his wife didn't accompany him on the walk-through to make sure we had everything she wanted done detailed in our work order?" Kaitlin asked. "I sure wouldn't leave it up to my husband to check off all the boxes I wanted checked so the place suited me."

"The woman who sleeps with vipers will die regretting it." Victoria chimed in. "I mean, if Thomas were my husband, the only thing I'd want to spend time with is his bank account. That man is like a cream puff—looks scrumptious on the outside but filled with pureed Brussel sprouts on the inside."

"Victoria, it always scares me when what you say actually plants a way too accurate picture in my mind." Ivy looked down, shaded her eyes with her hand, and shook her head. "Another thing that's going to be stuck in my brain for a while, but you've described him to a 'T'."

"Yeah, the first bite of that cream puff and I'd be spitting it out," said Serenity.

"It also bothered me that the son was listed as the title holder through some corporation on the deed. I thought Thomas was the only one who owned property for the firm," Jess said.

"I agree. It is odd, but the title report came back clean so it must be fine," Ivy said.

Jess tucked her clipboard under her arm. "What do you all say to taking the rest of the day off to celebrate?"

"You got my vote," Serenity said. "And I volunteer my family's winery for an afternoon of debauchery."

"Everyone in?" Jess asked. Victoria and Ivy nodded.

"Let me check with my mom to make sure she can pick up Joey from preschool." Kaitlin stepped away and after a minute on the phone, returned. "The kiddo's squared away, so I'm all set. When do we leave?"

"Why don't we meet out there around noon? Does that give everyone time to tie up loose ends?" Murmurs of assent followed.

"Noon it is." Serenity pulled out her phone. "I'll let my mom know. You guys know the drill. Get ready for full-on Italian hospitality."

THEY'D ELECTED TO DRIVE separately since they'd each be heading off in different directions once their half-day of playing hooky ended. Jess enjoyed the drive east of Sacramento along the rural roads into the area's wine country. Small towns and exclusive gated communities dotted the route of rolling hills and oak trees. The solitude provided time for reflection and cleared her mind of the mundane workday clutter. The conversation she'd had with her dad yesterday kept spinning in her head. After a few glasses of wine, Jess knew her friends would help her sort through it all.

Stepping out of her truck in the parking lot of *Bacieto dal Sol*, Jess let her gaze travel over the neat rows of vines in the nearby vineyard and the rustic, wood-sided tasting room building with its attached deck. The winery, owned and operated by Serenity's extended family, was into its third generation under Gagliardi management. Serenity's dad, Lorenzo, was the current patriarch. He co-owned the operation with his two brothers, Mateo and Diego, and two sisters, Francesca and Maria. By the time Jess added in the various spouses and their offspring, she felt like she needed to carry around a genealogy chart to keep them all straight.

Serenity's mom, Sophia, bustled out of the tasting room and engulfed Jess in a hug that left her struggling for breath. Finally released and held at arms' length, she waited for Sophia's standard pronouncement.

"You look too skinny. Come. Come. I have food for you. We'll fatten you up." Even though Sophia had spent her entire adulthood in California, the old country mannerisms remained. As a young man, Lorenzo had made a trip to Italy to visit family and returned with a bride. With an arm around Jess' shoulders and Jess's arm around Sophia's waist, the matriarch led her into a side room off the main tasting room.

Jess liked her body just fine and didn't see the need to change anything about her shape unless she could add four or five inches to her height. "Thank you, Mama Sophia. Your food is always delicious. I'm sure I'll walk away with a few extra pounds." Serenity's mom beamed. The quickest way to an Italian mother's heart was to praise her cooking. "I have dreams about your homemade pasta."

"Then you're in luck. I have the antipasto platter waiting. I follow that with lasagna and an *insalata* with greens fresh from the garden. Next *Formaggi e Frutta*. I picked up some lovely cheeses from our supplier and the apples and pears right from our trees..." She kissed her fingertips. "*Il perfetto*."

"Don't suppose there'll be any cannoli?" Jess' taste buds went into overdrive at the thought of her favorite dessert—especially Mama Sophia's.

"Made a batch this morning right after Serenity called."

"You are my hero." Jess squeezed Sophia's waist and broke away to join Serenity, Victoria, and Ivy at the tall, round bar table.

"I have a few more things to do in the kitchen, but then I'll join you so you can tell me everything that's going on in your lives." Sophia set another bottle of Pinot Noir on the table and left the room.

"You know that's mom speak for, '*if you plan to talk about something you don't want me to hear, do it now*'." Serenity plucked a slice of prosciutto from the platter and laid it across a piece of crostini.

"Where's Kaitlin? She's usually not late." Jess poured herself a glass of wine.

"Her mom waylaid her so she could show her the social media profile of one of her Bunco buddy's sons." Victoria bit into a slice of fresh fig drizzled with honey. "That lady's intent on finding a daddy for Joey and adding another grandbaby to her collection."

"She only has one grandchild," observed Ivy.

Victoria shrugged. "A collection has to start somewhere."

"I'll bet she just loves it when her mom tries to play matchmaker," Ivy snorted.

"Is that sarcasm I hear in your voice?" Kaitlin sailed in, full steam ahead. "And no, she does not want her mom picking out her next husband. Someone pour me a glass of wine. Did I miss anything?"

"Not yet." Victoria handed her an empty glass and a full bottle of wine. "We were just getting ready to grill Jess about her date with Devin on Saturday before Mama Sophia rejoins us to..." Victoria made air quotes, "*catch up on our lives.*"

"And most likely all the aunts too. Nothing they like better than a good gossip." Serenity rolled her eyes but a soft smile played around her lips. "It seems moms everywhere have the same goal... to butt into their children's lives."

"Not every mom." A pinch of envy blew its cold breath on Jess' heart, shrinking the contentment that had nested there to the size of a hummingbird egg. "My mom is strictly hands off.

"I'll trade you one tiger mom." Victoria pretended to select a card from the imaginary hand she held.

"Until you've had to deal with a large Italian family that the dictionary uses as an example to define meddling, you're just amateurs." Serenity pretended to toss a chip into the table. "Privacy isn't in their vocabulary."

"I'll see your meddlers and raise you one who wants to smother the life out of you." Ivy spread her hands out like she was positioning cards on the table. "*Honey, don't you need a coat? Your dad says you need new windshield wipers. Would you like him to go get them for you?* Sheesh, I'm thirty-two. I can take care of myself."

"I've got you all beat. One helicopter mom wins the pot." Kaitlin scooped up the imaginary chips and leveled a steady gaze at Jess. "And I'll throw in all the guys she's trying to set me up with for free."

Jess held up her hands in surrender. "No, thank you." While wistfulness whispered in her ear she added, "I guess we all want what we don't have."

"Speaking of wanting what we don't have, what's up with you and Devin? Your eyes light up whenever you mention him." Kaitlin pointed a finger at Jess. "And that blush. That's new."

"Damn fair skin. I can't hide anything." Jess took a fortifying sip of wine. She still felt guilty about dating an employee but couldn't stop the grin that told her friends exactly what she felt inside. Soft as a cotton ball. "It was nice."

"Nice? Nice is for a dress you sort of like." Victoria tapped her fingernail on the table. "Nice is not how you describe a guy so hot I expect you to go up in flames. Nice is not how you describe a guy who makes you act all first-crush squishy." She wagged her finger in the air like a pendulum. "How does he make you feel? Really feel."

"Am I supposed to emote, and gesticulate, and reveal my deepest desires?"

"You know it. That's what friends do." Kaitlin's solemn expression didn't hide the humor in her eyes. "And we want details. Don't leave anything out. Are you madly, ravishingly in love? Make us swoon." She put two hands over her heart and slumped in her chair.

The group erupted in laughter. Once they'd all wiped the tears from their faces, Serenity topped off everyone's glass.

Heat crawled up Jess' neck and she had to resist the urge to pat her cheeks. "I don't have the words, or at least I don't think I can say them out loud, to describe the swoon-worthy performance of Devin."

She held up her hands to the chorus of groans from her companions. "What I can say is that he does make my lady parts beg for more. I never thought of myself as an overly sexual being. I like sharing intimacy with my partners but it wasn't like I couldn't wait to be with any of them again. Devin's different."

A collective sigh floated around the table like a gentle breeze and her friends shifted in their seats.

"Just looking at that man gets me all wet." Victoria ran her tongue along her upper teeth. "Are those lips of his as luscious as they look? I'll bet he's a great kisser."

Jess felt her eyes go wide and she exhaled a long, slow breath. "Oh yes." She smiled and fluttered her lashes. "Dream on, ladies." Growing serious, she continued. "I like being with him." A giggle wiggled its way up her chest. "And it's not just the fantastic sex." She glanced around the table at the expectant faces. "You asked how he makes me feel. Alive. Happy. At ease. I can tell him anything, which is a real change for me. He makes me feel like a woman but also an equal partner in the relationship. I trust him. Again, another novel feeling for me. It's eye-opening to realize a man can make me feel this way."

"Aw Jess. We're happy for you." Kaitlin jumped off her stool. "Group hug." Jess thought her heart would burst from all the love hovering in the air.

When they returned to their seats, Ivy asked, "What's next for the two of you?"

"I don't know, but for once I'm eager to find out."

The door between the kitchen and the extension to this tasting room swung open. Mama Sophia swept in bearing the lasagna, followed by two of the aunts, one carrying the salad and the other a bottle of wine in each hand. They set the feast on the rectangular patio table along the side wall by the large window with the view of the vineyard.

Serenity rose and greeted each of her aunts with a kiss on each cheek. "*Zia* Francesca. *Zia* Maria. So nice to see you."

Francesca wagged a finger at Serenity. "We were beginning to think you had forgotten us." The scold ended with a smile and a hug. "How is that *bambina* of yours? Her cousins miss her."

"She started playing on the league soccer team which means more after-school practices and more games on the weekend. Life is busy once children get serious about sports... and she's taking piano lessons." Serenity put a hand on Francesca's arm. "But I will make a point of getting her out here soon. I also want to freshen up the flower boxes with cooler weather plants."

Mama Sophia asked after each of the partner's families. In Italian culture, the child didn't have friends—*the families had friends*. They expected to know the parents of each of their children's playmates and everybody's business.

When it was Jess' turn, Mama Sophia asked, "Are things any better between you and your father?"

"I had dinner with them yesterday and strangely enough, I think Dad is starting to come around."

"Well, that's a good thing. No?" *Zia* Francesca said.

"It is. While I don't think he'll ever be happy that I'm in construction, at least I don't feel like such a disappointment. I have a better understanding of where he's coming from. He's afraid I'll get hurt and wants to protect me."

*Zia* Maria reached over and squeezed Jess' hand. "That is only natural. That is what God put fathers and mothers on this earth to do. To take care of their children. Keep them from harm." She lifted one shoulder in a European way.

"But until this weekend I believed there was nothing I could do to be good enough. It was like he was jealous of who I had become and I didn't know what to do about that." Jess tunneled her fingers through her hair which she had let hang loose. "Even though I see his perspective more clearly, it still hurts. The only thing I've wanted was for him to be proud of me." Jess couldn't believe she was saying this but it had reached the point where she couldn't keep it bottled up anymore.

Mama Sophia stood, and, pulling Jess from her chair, gathered her in her arms. The soft pats on the back brought comfort and so did Mama Sophia's words. "Parents are not perfect and sometimes disappointments from our own lives spills onto our children. That's not fair, I know." She held Jess at arm's length. "But you, Jessica

Winters, are a strong woman. You don't need anyone's approval to be *fantastico...* a vibrant, kind, caring, and determined young woman." Mama Sophia made a motion for Jess to sit. "Now I think it is time for more wine and cannoli."

On the drive home, Jess reflected on the collective wisdom and came to the conclusion that it was in Victoria's words, *about damn time you realized you were enough*. No one's disapproval could take away her respect. She should be proud of who she was and what she'd built. From here on out, she planned to live that belief.

# Chapter Eighteen

THE CALL SURPRISED Devin. Even though they spoke often, this was different. She wanted to see him... tonight... at his new apartment. He'd moved in two weeks ago and this was the first time she'd expressed interest in seeing this side of his life. He'd always felt like she was holding a piece of herself back. Usually they went to her place, worked on one of her projects, and spent as much time as possible in her bed. Now she might end up in *his* bed. It might be an insignificant distinction to some, but to Devin it felt major.

She'd seemed exceptionally upbeat at work today—not that Jess would ever wear her emotions on her sleeve. That would be unprofessional. He knew Uniquely Yours had closed a big remodel deal yesterday but the way she'd kept glancing at him when no one else was looking, must mean something.

At least he hoped so.

So much was changing. He'd made arrangements to talk to an attorney in a few days about potential blowback on himself and his siblings. When they all got together next week during Madison's visit, he'd share what he learned. They were all involved in the tangled mess their father had created and should have a say in how to proceed.

Devin would wait and tell Jess who he was and why he'd come here until after he'd met with his brother and sister. He and Jess seemed to have entered a new phase in their relationship and he wasn't looking forward to disrupting their bond. He also didn't know exactly how he'd break the news but he'd work out something.

She'd be here any minute. He carefully placed the silverware on the cloth napkins. Stood back and examined the arrangement. Didn't the fork go on the napkin and the knife and spoon on the other side? He moved the spoon and knife. He adjusted the flowers he'd picked up for the table to make sure they were centered. Scooched the candles a little farther away from the flowers and then moved them back.

He slapped his forehead with the heel of his hand. What was he doing? He'd spent a half hour putting together an appropriate playlist of romantic songs for background music. That's what adults did. Right? He sighed and closed his eyes. No, he was acting like a man in love—or at least the way he thought a man in love would act. That was another thing he and Jess needed to talk about. So far they'd only danced around the subject.

Devin jumped at the knock on his door. Smoothing his hands down his jean-clad thighs, he hustled to the door. She stood on the landing. A slow smile spread across his face. She had on makeup. Her blonde hair must have seen the business end of a curling iron, because a riot of soft curls framed her face. She'd wiggled into a pair of skinny, black jeans that he had every intention of peeling off her at the first opportunity. A short, white top that didn't quite reach her waistband offered a glimpse of creamy skin. A cardigan sweater protected her from the evening chill.

Capturing her hand, he pulled her inside and into his arms. Kicking the door shut, his lips made a beeline for hers. He only drew away when his lungs demanded that he gulp in a large dose of air to satisfy his pounding heart. The intoxicating scent of the same exotic perfume she'd worn to the nightclub slammed his overheated system into overdrive. Was this a special occasion?

"God, you're beautiful." Propping one hand flat against the door, his other hand cradled her head. Instinctively, his fingers tangled in her hair when his lips couldn't resist another taste. A mouth he couldn't get enough of and that sent him to a place of bright colors and flashing lights.

Soft fingers pressed into his cheeks and gently put a hair's breadth of distance between them. "I think you promised me some dinner. If you want more of this..." Her tongue traced his lips and almost brought him to his knees. "You're going to have to keep your promise."

"I definitely want more of this." His finger followed the neckline of her top. Her shiver sent electric shockwaves coursing through his body. Taking her hand in his, he led her toward the tiny, galley kitchen. "I put a roast in the crock pot this morning so I can offer sustenance. Among other things."

"It smells wonderful." As they passed the square wooden table ringed with four folding chairs, she bent and pressed her nose to the flowers.

The twinkle in her eyes when she straightened made him feel like he was king of the world.

"You've outdone yourself. I'm touched." Jess fingered the placemat he'd arranged with such care on the table. "Cloth napkins and all. Can I do anything to help?"

"I've got it under control. Why don't you take a seat?" After lighting the candles, he carried the ceramic liner from the crock pot to the table and set it on a folded towel. From the fridge, he retrieved the salad and another bottle of Pellegrino. Satisfied, he took a seat across from her. "Help yourself."

"Where did you learn to cook like this?" She waved her hands over the bowl and inhaled.

"In rehab, we all had chores. I ended up in the kitchen and discovered I liked it. Gave me a chance to experiment with textures and flavors. Turns out I have a knack for it."

"Did you ever consider becoming a chef?"

A jolt of electricity rocketed through him at the look of pleasure that crossed her face when she bit into a chunk of meat. A drop of gravy clung to her lips and he started to rise to lick it off but her napkin beat him to it. His lips curled in a grin at the glint of humor in her eyes.

"Are you toying with me?" A come hither tilt to her lips was the only answer he got. "No. Being cooped up eight to ten hours a day in a hot, busy kitchen? Not how I want to live my life. An hour or so puttering and getting to eat the fruits of my labor... that's another story."

"It's the culinary world's loss but my gain. I'm happy you're part of my crew. You have a knack for construction as well. You have a future there if you want it."

"Thank you ma'am." He felt heat rise up his neck and hoped she didn't notice. "Hear you have a big project on the horizon."

"Escrow opened this morning. I turned in the application for the permits. Kaitlin's ordering the supplies and my crew will start demolition on Monday. It's a huge mansion on an acre of land. The guy wants it completely updated, a sauna added to the master bath, a guest house built, new landscaping, tennis courts, the works. It could get our toe in the water of the luxury home market."

"Don't we have to finish the Jackson Street flip before starting a new job?"

"Rollo's red team just finished the Bridgeport Way flip so I'm thinking about moving them over to ours so my crew can start on the new project. Or his crew can start on the new home construction for my sister's house. Or I can promote Bryan to foreman and give him his own crew and let him take on the new construction project. So many moving parts."

"Busy is good, right?"

Propping her elbows on the table, she rested her chin on her hands. "Yes, busy is good but only if I keep the quality of our work up. I'm so afraid of letting something slip through the cracks. Ivy has another house in escrow that will close in about four weeks and one of the crews will need to start work on that one."

Devin watched her worry her bottom lip. He pushed his empty plate away and stood. "For what it's worth, I think Bryan is ready." He came around the table and put his hands on her shoulders and kissed the top of her head. "Just remember, you have a team around you. People who believe in you." His lips strayed to the back of her neck. "You'll make the right decision."

He stepped back as she stood. "Should we clean up the kitchen?"

She turned in his arms and her hands smoothed up his chest. "I suggest you give me a tour of you apartment, starting with your bedroom. We can take care of the dishes after we've had dessert."

He took her hand in his and brought it to his lips. "It's not much. I haven't had time to do any decorating."

"Don't let Victoria hear you say that. She'll be on you like a flea on a dog. The only reason I have matching furniture is because of her." Jess squeezed his hand. "It makes me feel all grown up to have the rooms I've finished decorated and ready for company."

He watched her gaze take in his second-hand sofa, end table, and battered bookcase. The only new items were the recliner and a wall-mounted television. He didn't see disgust or dismay. Slowly he released the breath he'd been holding.

"Looks comfortable. Like a place where a person could relax. I like it."

Leading her into the bedroom, where his king-size bed dominated the space, he pulled her into his arms again. "Nothing fancy here, but I did try out a lot of beds before I settled on this one. Drove the salesman crazy. I think you'll like it."

"With you in it, there's no doubt."

He brought a lock of her hair to his nose and breathed in her intoxicating scent. "Jess, you bring me to my knees." Lightly skimming her shoulders, he eased her sweater down her arms until it floated to the floor.

"Devin." His name sat on her lips like a plea. "Make love to me." Her clear blue eyes turned the color of a storm-tossed sea.

Slowly. Patiently. He splayed his hands at her waist and under her top loving the feel of her soft skin under his palms. With a steadiness that surprised him since his heart beat like a jackhammer, he eased his hands along her ribs taking the top with him. She raised her arms so he could slip it off. She moaned as his hands caressed her arms, first up to remove the top, and then back down. He bent his head and trailed a string of kisses on the swell above her bra.

Cupping her breasts in his hands, he admired the delicate scrap of material that contained them. "I don't think I've seen you in something so lacy. Is it new?"

She answered with a kiss that rattled his brain.

On a groan of pleasure he asked, "For me?"

"Only you." A blush tinged her cheeks and she lowered her lashes. "I wanted to wear something special. Feminine and pretty."

A chuckle rumbled from his chest. "Even in your work boots and hardhat, there's not a man alive who'd doubt you're a woman. But you have added an interesting twist to the job site. Now I'm going to have to wonder every day what's under your work clothes."

She waggled her brows and grinned. That grin quickly morphed into an expression of pleasure when his hands feathered down her body. Her eyes closed and she swayed in his arms as inch by inch he explored the dips and curves of her perfect body. Unsnapping and then very leisurely unzipping her jeans, he guided them over her hips. He knelt in front of her, burying his nose in the taut skin of her belly, and worked the fabric down her legs.

Holding her hips, he instructed, "Sit."

She obeyed, a tremble in the hand on his shoulder. His pulse scampered like a hare being chased by hounds. Reverently, he raised her leg so he could remove one strappy, high-heel sandal. He kissed her ankle and gently nipped the soft flesh at the top of her foot. He repeated the process with her other foot and then finished removing her jeans. Taking her hands in his, he pulled her to stand in front of him. His hands cupped her ass. Her breath came in pants.

Don't rush. Take your time. The commands filled his brain.

He wanted to drag out every moment of pleasure that he could. Savor the miracle of Jess in his arms. A miracle he might not deserve but one he would treasure for as long as he lived.

He wanted to offer her everything that he was. He wanted to tease her and touch her until the sensation of their love-making was her only reality. Until she was swept away in a sea of passion. Hooking his thumbs in her panties, he eased them down her legs until she could step out of them. His tongue laved and circled the hard nub at the V of her legs. Moist and ready, his fingers entered her and caressed the spot that had her moaning in pleasure until the contractions let him know she had spiraled over the edge.

"Oh God," she said as her knees buckled. He nudged her onto the bed. Spurred by the desire rushing through his veins, he quickly disposed of his clothing and eased on top of her. Her hands fisted in his hair and she took his mouth in a desperate kiss. His blood pounded in his ears and his cock ached to be inside her. Soon enough he would grant himself that wish.

Taking her breast into his mouth he shuddered at the feel of her damp skin sliding against his and her heart thudding in unison with his under his cheek. No matter what else happened in his life, he would have this moment. Reaching for the bedside table, he pulled a condom from the drawer and rolled it on.

She lifted her hips inviting him to join with her. They moved together, the pressure building. He drove them higher with long, slow strokes. The rising and falling of exquisite tension. The blinding white light. Their bodies quaking from the intensity of the sensation. When the release hit, thunder and lightning exploded in his brain. Breathing seemed optional but he gulped in air anyway before collapsing on her in a shuddering heap.

Once they could move they lay on their sides, facing each other. A soft smile played on her lips. "That was some dessert." Jess' tongue circled her lips. "I may want seconds."

"You can have as many helpings as you want." His finger traced the delicate shell of her ear. "Though you may have to give me a few minutes." He shivered and drew in a quick breath when she traced a finger down his sternum. Snagging her finger and kissing it, he asked, "How was your girl get-away yesterday?"

"Really nice. I think we need to do more of that. We all tend to get caught up in our work to the detriment of our social lives." Jess lifted to her elbow and propped her head on her hand. "This is turning out to be some week. On Sunday, my dad and I called a truce. Wonder of wonders, he said that while he's not thrilled I'm in the construction business, he admitted I'm doing a good job."

Devin leaned in and kissed her. "That's great. Looks like we're both making some headway with our families."

"You've made up with your parents?"

He could hear the excitement in her voice and hated to put a damper on it. "No, nothing that drastic. But I've seen my brother a few times and there's a definite thaw happening. My sister arrives next week for a visit and the three of us will get together. I count the three of us in the same room as progress."

"Looks like we both have something to celebrate." She walked her fingers up his arm. "You ready for some more dessert?"

Scooping her into his arms, he leaped back into heaven.

# Chapter Nineteen

"THIS IS WHERE Philip lives? He's done well for himself." Madison lowered the visor on the passenger side of Devin's truck and touched up her lipstick. She fluffed her long, dark, curly hair before stepping onto the circular driveway.

"It would appear Dad's paying our little brother well." Devin glanced up at the imposing, two story, Colonial-style home. Forest green shutters framed the windows that were symmetrically aligned on either side of the house. The steps leading to the front door were sheltered by a peaked pediment. It was a pleasant, orderly house—just like Philip.

"And you don't think he has any idea how deep into the weeds Dad has gone?" She smoothed her hands down her faux leather skirt and tugged on the neckline of her scoop-neck black sweater as they waited at the front door.

"No, I don't think he does. Every time I brought up Dad's illicit activities, he shot me down. It's as though he'd rather not know. I get that. No one wants to believe bad things about their parents." He ran his fingers through his hair. "Now that I have actual proof about what's going on, I hope he'll be more receptive and cover his..." He stopped speaking when the front door opened.

"Hi Shelly." As usual her infectious grin brought out his own. Phil was one lucky guy. His wife radiated a love and contentment that their own parents had lacked. That boded well for the family they would raise. "Thanks for inviting us over."

"Are you kidding? I'm thrilled to have the chance to meet Phil's sister." Shelly stepped back and ushered them in. "Phil will join us in a few minutes. He's on a call. Can't tell you how excited he is to see you again, Madison." She chattered on as she led them into the living room. "Where are my manners?" She took a breath and extended her hand. "I'm Shelly, Phil's wife. Now that we've been formally intro-duced..." She embraced her sister-in-law a quick hug.

"I'm glad to have the chance to meet you too." Madison glanced around. "You have a lovely home. Have you lived here long?"

"Only about a year." She placed a hand on her baby bump. "We wanted to raise our children in a family-friendly neighborhood. The house Thomas and Carla insisted we buy when we first married was a bit too..." She paused, apparently searching for the right word. "...for-mal for our tastes."

Madison snorted. "I think the word you really meant was *snooty*."

Shelly giggled. "Yeah, that's the word I meant. We wanted a neigh-borhood filled with kids and a house we wouldn't care if they messed up." She looked around her. "And while this is still more pretentious that we wanted, in families, you do have to make compromises."

175

"As long as those compromises don't cross any ethical boundaries, then I agree," Madison said.

Devin didn't miss Shelly's assessing look. He wondered how much she knew.

His sister reached out and gently patted Shelly's belly. "When are you due?"

Shelly sighed. "Another two months."

"Hi all. Sorry I was tied up." Phil strode into the room, slapped Devin on the back, and then swept Madison up in a big bear hug. "Sis, it's good to see you again." When he released her, he stepped back and looked her up and down. "When you left for college, I'd just started junior high. All I remember is my gorgeous big sister who I looked up to. Not much has changed." He swept her up in another hug.

"I've missed you too. You're not a kid anymore." Madison patted his cheek. "I'm sorry you all missed my graduation... both of them. Devin was there. It would have been nice to have had the rest of the family present."

"It's such a nice day. I love October," Shelly broke in. "I thought we'd have lunch on the patio. Why don't we go out there and get settled and catch up?" She linked her arm through her husband's and nudged him forward.

Devin trailed behind the group wanting to assess the dynamics. He hadn't been sure how the reunion would go. Maybe a little tense, but all in all, not bad. Could have been so much worse. Philip obviously wanted to reconnect with Madison. They were a long way from best buddies, but they both seemed willing to try.

They stepped out onto a large section of earth-toned pavers. A long, patio table and several umbrellas sat to their left. A fairly extensive outdoor kitchen carved out a space on their right. A massive manicured lawn dotted with old trees and ringed with shrubs and flower gardens stretched out for about an acre. A fenced-in pool sat about 20 yards to the right.

"You must spend a lot of time out here," Madison observed.

"We do," Shelly said. "I love to garden, and Phil has become quite the outdoor chef."

"I've developed some great rubs for the meat." Phil held out a chair for Shelly. "I'll be grilling my famous chicken for lunch."

"Sounds yummy." Madison accepted the chair that Devin held for her.

"Look, I'm going to shoo the eight-hundred pound gorilla out of the room right now." Shelly rested her forearms on the table, her hands splayed palms up in supplication, and she shrugged. "I know a lot of the bad blood between you is the result of your estrangement from Thomas. I hear you're concerned that Phil might get caught up in something that Thomas is doing and I'd like to hear your side."

Out of the corner of his eye, Devin watched Phil's reaction. Straight face. The two of them must have planned this. Nice move. And there was that glance they'd exchanged. They were a team.

"I like a woman who gets to the point," Madison said. "Devin's been doing some investigating and has turned up some disturbing information." She waved her hand, indicating Devin should take over.

"I completely understood your reluctance to take my word about my suspicions, so I set out to get some proof. Rumors floated around the construction industry, but that might have been nothing more than disgruntled business owners with a grudge, and I wasn't sure anyone would talk to me anyway. When a search of public records didn't turn up any lawsuits or mechanics liens, I was stumped for a while. Then I remembered Ellen Bitterman." He looked at Phil. "You remember her? The company's CFO?"

"Yeah, she left the firm when her son got sick. Dad kept her on as a consultant and even put her son on the payroll so he'd get health insurance." Phil made a face. "I thought that was pretty decent of Dad."

"There's more to the story than that." Devin rested his arms on his thighs and leaned forward. He needed Phil to really hear this. "Years ago, during a routine audit, Ellen turned up paperwork that didn't look right." Devin spent the next half hour sharing what he'd learned from Ellen. "I made a copy of the thumb drive she gave me so you can see the documents for yourself."

Phil looked stunned as he reached for the small device. He examined it like it might bite him. "Thanks, I think. This is a lot to take in."

"I wish that were all. When I was checking the public records for the companies Ellen found that were in my name, I noticed the same name appeared as the registered agent on all the documents. Not only that, all the companies used the same business address. It took some digging but I found that by searching on that guy's name in the state where these businesses were incorporated that he popped up all over the place. I thought that was strange. The same guy was also the registered agent on businesses in your name and Madison's name."

"Wait." Phil put his hands flat on the table and stood up. "There are businesses in my name? That aren't connected to TLM Investments?"

"Afraid so. All this is way above my pay grade so a friend hooked me up with an attorney. He told me that it looks like Dad set up a bunch of shell companies. While shell companies aren't necessarily illegal, they can be used for illegal purposes—like hiding assets, evading taxes, buying property you don't want anyone to know about—all kinds of things."

"But how did this go undetected for so long?" Phil asked. "I mean, I file tax returns. Why hasn't this raised red flags at the IRS?" He sat back down and slumped in his chair.

"Because shell companies are designed to keep the owners anonymous. Everything goes to the registered agent and the public facing documents all list the registered agent. My name had been left on the articles of incorporation that Ellen found. That's what got me started uncovering the truth." Devin ran a hand over his hair. "At any rate, the attorney said that if Dad is involved in illegal activities and has been doing it in our names without our knowledge, that's identity theft. If we want to keep ourselves out of legal trouble, we need to take all this to the authorities and let them figure out what's going on."

Phil clasped his hands in his lap and blew out a long breath. Shelly got up and put her hands on her husband's shoulders. "Give me a few days to review all this and I'll get back to you. You won't do anything until then?"

"I can give you a few days, but I'd hoped we could all meet with the attorney before Madison leaves." Devin could see the tension in his brother's jaw. "I'm sorry about all this. I really wish none of this was true." Devin felt hollow inside. He hated turning his brother's world upside down.

"What will all this mean for Dad and for TLM Investments?" Phil asked.

"I'm not sure. Depending upon what the authorities turn up... maybe nothing, maybe fines, maybe prison. My guess is TLM Investments won't survive if it's proved that Dad is involved in illegal activities."

"And what about Ellen? Couldn't she end up getting caught in the crossfire?" Phil bit his lip. "She's a nice lady and I was sorry about her son."

Phil's question convinced Devin his brother had nothing to do with all of this. He cared about people. "Ellen and I talked, and she's ready to face whatever legal repercussions come her way. She wants to get everything out in the open."

Phil patted his wife's hand. "When all the shit hits the fan, it's a good thing I've got a backup career plan. Teaching's something I always wanted to do anyway." He looked over the yard. "We might lose all this though."

Shelly bent and kissed her husband's cheek. "That's fine by me. I'm married to you, not this place. As long as we're together, we'll be fine."

A pressure built in Devin's chest. "Part of me is sorry I uncovered all this and what it's going to mean for each of our lives. I suspect we'll be spending a lot of time with attorneys. Part of me is glad, since stuff like this usually comes to light at some point. At least this way, we'll have time to be proactive and minimize the damage."

Phil ran a hand through his hair. "I agree. If what you've uncovered is illegal, I don't want any part of it." He stood again. "Anyone hungry? I think it's time to fire up the grill." Amid nervous laughter, he did just that.

# Chapter Twenty

"WELCOME TO OUR NEW Floral Road project." Jess stood in a wide stance holding her clipboard at her side. She had assembled her crew to outline the scope of the work they'd be doing for Thomas Miller and introduce new members of the team. "We'll be doing an extensive remodel to the main house along with building a guest house. The remodel also includes a major addition to the master bedroom and bath plus extending the kitchen out into the interior courtyard." She slapped the clipboard against her leg. "This is a big deal for us and will go a long way to raising our profile in the region. I'll walk you through today's tasks in a few minutes. Any questions?"

Everyone shook their heads, but their grins told her they were excited to get started.

"Before we get underway, I'm sure you've noticed that Bryan is missing. I'm happy to announce he's been promoted to crew foreman. He'll head up our new orange team and finish up the flip you were just working on. After he wraps that, his team will start on our next flip. Rollo's team will start work on a new home construction project next week. As you can see, we've got quite a bit of work in the pipeline."

She waited for the applause and whistles to die down. "Next, I'd like to introduce you to our newest team members, Ed Burrows and Hank Mason. Please introduce yourself to them and make them feel welcome."

After the handshakes and introductions finished, Jess continued. "I've also brought over Seth Yarnell from Rollo's red team until we get everything framed in. Hopefully, most of you know him from our annual picnic. If you don't, make sure you introduce yourself. Now if you'll all follow me. The house is just over 7,500 square feet. The owner won't be living here until construction is complete so we have the run of the place..."

An hour later she had one team doing demo in the kitchen and a second team opening walls between the living room and dining room before they moved on to do the prep work for the master bedroom and bathroom expansion. Jess loved demo day. Not only was it cathartic—a chance to work out any frustrations with a solid *thwack* with a sledgehammer against a wall—but it brought everything down to the bare bones. From there it was a vast palette of possibilities. There was also the added benefit of watching Devin work, his muscles rippling and bunching across his broad back.

He caught her ogling him and grinned. She quickly looked away, feeling a bit like a school girl peeking around the corner of the gym to catch a glimpse of the guys at football practice. He wandered over but kept a respectful distance. She was grateful that through his stance and demeanor he made it look like he had only approached her to ask a question.

Devin pitched his voice low so it wouldn't carry beyond her ears. "Glad I can provide you with some entertainment." His words drifted across her skin like silk and an anticipatory shiver whispered down her spine.

Jess swung her arm as though explaining the next phase of the task and matched the pitch of her voice to his. "Don't you know that I only keep you around as eye candy?"

He nodded and kept his expression neutral, but his tone was teasing. "You wound me. And here I thought you respected me. Hard to swallow that I'm only a piece of meat." Raising his voice so the others could hear, he said, "Okay boss. After we finish making the arch frame for this wall we'll move on to prep for the master bedroom and bath addition."

Jess was tempted to pinch that tight butt of his as he walked away but didn't want to draw the attention of the rest of the team. "Don't forget to remove the existing grass and scrape down to the dirt, then bring the dirt up to grade and pack it." She raised one finger. "Oh, and Serenity's crew should already have removed the plants that were next to the house. If that hasn't happened, let me know."

"Will do." He sauntered off giving her another opportunity to enjoy the view. She wasn't sure she was fooling anyone but she had to at least pretend theirs was only a business relationship. For now. Devin had earned the respect of the rest of her crew. The time was coming when she could make the fact they were dating public. She had mixed feelings about that. Part of her wanted to keep her growing attachment to him to herself to savor. Another part wanted the world to know Devin loved her.

She raised her voice and spoke to his retreating back. "We'll add the rebars and moisture barrier tomorrow after the plumber is finished.

We'll need to hustle because the concrete guys arrive in two days. I'm going to check on the kitchen demo now."

He waved his hand at the back of his head to acknowledge he'd heard.

"And even though my back is turned, I want you to keep those hardhats on." She pivoted and raised her brows staring down the group scowling at her. "Just remember, a guy in a hardhat is sexy." She exited the room to catcalls and groans.

In the kitchen, Jess surveyed the room. Jamal, Penny, Jeremy, and Seth had already managed to carefully detach all the upper cabinets and deposit them in their hauling trailer. With the owner's permission they always donated the useable materials to a local housing for the homeless organization. At the moment Jamal and Seth were wrestling the dishwasher out of its nook and Jeremy was strapping the refrigerator to a hand truck. Penny had a crowbar under one edge of the sink.

Jess slipped on her work gloves and grabbed another crowbar. "Let me help."

"Thanks, Jess. This'll go much faster with an extra set of hands."

As they carried it out to the dumpster, Jess asked, "So you and Jamal have worked out your differences?"

"Yeah, we're all squared away. Funny the silly things couples fight about."

"How so?" They heaved the heavily chipped cast iron sink in the dumpster and dusted off their gloved hands.

"Damn, that thing's heavy. This place is a mess. You'd think someone who lived in this neighborhood would take care of their property."

"The new owner bought it in foreclosure. I guess the people who lost it didn't care about upkeep. I'm surprised the appliances and cabinets were still intact."

Penny pulled off her gloves and tucked them into her back pocket. "The argument started because I wanted to go out with my girlfriends and he thought we'd be trolling for guys. I told him that wasn't going to happen but he wouldn't believe me. He insisted that I go out with him instead. I told him to take a hike."

They each grabbed a bottle of water out of the cooler. Jess tilted her head back and chugged a third of the bottle. "So how did you finally end your quarrel?" She screwed the cap back on. "Sorry if I'm being too nosy. You don't need to answer if you don't want to."

Penny grinned. "I don't mind. We're all family after all." She sipped her water. "He apologized when he realized what an ass he was being. Karma's a bitch. A few days later, he wanted to go out with the guys and I asked if he planned to pick up another woman." Penny chuckled. "You've never seen someone back pedal as fast as he did. He got the message. Just because we do things with our friends that don't include our partner, doesn't mean we forget who our heart belongs to."

"Amen to that one. Jealousy can wreak havoc on a relationship." Jess felt Penny's eyes on her.

"We've moved in together," Penny said.

"It's serious then?" Jess stopped and leaned against the garage wall and crossed her arms.

"Looks that way. We've met each other's parents, and Jamal hinted that I should expect a special present for Christmas."

"What's it like living and working together? Is it weird?" A tight knot formed in Jess' stomach. Could she and Devin date and still work together? They obviously still had a long way to go to before stepping into something permanent. The thought of Devin meeting her folks gave her the chills and his relationship with his family was sketchy at best. Plus she was the boss. Could that cause problems? At least Penny and Jamal were on the same playing field.

"It was at first." Penny rolled her eyes. "How we handled our first fight is a case in point. But we've made a pact that whatever happens at home, stays at home."

Jess pushed away from the wall and gave Penny a quick hug. "I'm happy for you two. I mean it. Congratulations."

Penny glanced at her feet and mumbled a thank you but Jess could see the blush creep into her cheeks. Ah, the first bloom of love. New and exciting and confusing. Jess placed her hand on Penny's shoulder. "I suppose we'd better get back to work before the guys accuse us of being slackers."

—ele—

DEVIN WIPED THE sweat out of his eyes with his arm. His back muscles ached but in a good way. Doing honest work gave a satisfaction he hadn't known was missing in his life. Scraping away the grass definitely got the heart rate going but was a necessary part of the process to ensure the integrity of the cement foundation that would be poured the day after tomorrow.

A slight breeze helped cool him. The morning had started out in the high forties but had already warmed into the low seventies. His sweatshirt, along with those of the other two guys working on this task, lay in a heap off to the side. Stepping over the two by fours pegged into place by stakes that made up the form for the foundation, he leaned on his shovel and studied the plot. Ed, who'd hauled away the last of the grass, showed up with a wheelbarrow full of dirt—the first of many—so they could bring the site up to grade. Hank followed, carrying three bottles of water.

"This section looks clean. Once we bring it up to grade we can run the compactor and then trench the sauna area for plumbing." Devin accepted a bottle of water from Hank. "How's the kitchen section looking?"

Out of the corner of his eye, he saw Jess step out of the house and he felt the kick of excitement that came with her presence.

"I pulled up the pavers in the courtyard and stacked them off to the side until Jess tells us what to do with them." Hank held the bottle against his cheek. "It's ready for us to build the forms. Do you want me to bring the plate compactor around?"

"That would be a yes," Jess said walking to where they were standing. "Ed, do you have experience working the compactor?"

The tall, lanky man with long rusty-colored hair that he'd gathered in a ponytail nodded. "Yes ma'am. I can handle that for you."

"Good." She pointed at Hank and Devin. "You two go tackle the kitchen expansion section. We need all the prep work done by tomorrow morning so the plumber can do his thing. I know it's a tight schedule but the weather forecast said we might get some rain next week. I'd like to get the concrete poured and give it a few days to cure before that."

"Guess we'd better get on it." Devin slung the shovel over his shoulder. "Do we have time to get all this done before the plumber gets here tomorrow?"

"The kitchen demo's finished inside so that team will work on the guest house foundation prep." Jess shaded her eyes and gazed to where the guest house would sit near the pool.

As Devin followed Ed around the corner of the building, he couldn't help calling back over his shoulder, "Good thing we loaded up plenty of shovels this morning. I think there's one with your name on it."

Jess' laughter scampered after him and affection bubbled in his chest.

"I have no doubt," she said. "Until we get this part of the job done, it's all hands on deck, including mine."

Devin and Ed had finished building the forms for the cement that would extend the foundation out from the house for the kitchen addition and had paused to guzzle some water when Hank rolled the plate compactor into the courtyard.

"Finished tamping down the soil in the bedroom and bath section with this beast." Hank swiped sweat from his neck with a rag. "At least you guys have had shade." He tucked the rag in his back pocket. "Ed, you and me are going to help get the guest house area ready. Devin, you get to run the compactor over this area and trench for the plumbing." The two guys left and Devin got to work.

He'd just turned off the compactor and removed his ear protectors and goggles when he heard a discrete cough. He glanced in the direction of the sound expecting to see one of the crew—or better yet—Jess. Everything inside him went still. Including his heart.

"Hello son. Moving up in the world I see. From derelict to laborer." Thomas Miller brushed nonexistent lint from his impeccable suit. *Just like he'd brushed his eldest son from his life.*

The sneer in his father's voice might as well have been a defibrillator. Devin's heart thudded back into action and blood rushed through his body. His hands fisted. Seeing his dad here caught him off guard. Unclenching his fists he looked down at his feet and counted to ten before answering. Devin hadn't known whose house this was. If he'd known, he might have tried to get reassigned or at least taken steps to keep out of his father's sight.

When Devin looked up, he stared straight into his father's eyes. "If you're intimating that I should feel shame for what I'm doing to make my living, too bad. What I do is honest work. I'm not like you. I don't cheat people." He could hardly spit the words out past the tightness in his chest.

Thomas shrugged. "And look where you are and then look where I am." He swept his arms out like a Ring Master addressing the audience. "You could have lived like this if you'd ditched your holier than thou attitude." Again he shrugged. "People who aren't smart enough to protect their interests, deserve what they get. They all knew who they were climbing into bed with. They had choices. "

"And the people who trample others under their feet? What do they get? I know what I heard and I know that Gerry Winters is one of the people you cheated." Devin felt heat crawl up his neck. A muscle ticked along his jaw. This man had no conscience. Not an ounce of remorse.

"They get power and wealth. They get people who bow and scrap and grovel just to be in the presence of the great one." Thomas' smile showed off a mouthful of perfectly capped teeth. "They get me and are happy to exist in my orbit hoping a little gold will fall off my tree and into their laps, including Winters."

"Is that why you got rid of me? Because I wasn't happy to exist in your orbit? I didn't care about your money?" Fury hit his chest like a blow torch, hot and targeted.

Thomas sighed. "Ever dramatic." He shook his head. "I suppose. That, and you were never going to be the son I wanted. The one to keep the empire I built growing. You were too busy trying to play by rules that other people set."

A hard freeze settled deep into Devin's bones. "And Philip? Is he the son you wanted? The one willing to step across the line of legality?"

"Not really. But at least he doesn't ask questions." Another shrug that set Devin's teeth on edge. "He's useful and puts an honest face on our image."

Devin rubbed the back of his neck. "So you're admitting to what I overheard as a kid? What happens if these guys finally decide to come after you?"

"They won't. Statute of limitations." Thomas narrowed his eyes and his stance became threatening. "And if the business ever does have problems, I'll do my best to take Philip, you, and Madison down with me."

Devin thought he heard a sound and glanced toward the hallway outside the courtyard. He didn't see anything. God, he was jumpy.

A few seconds later from somewhere in the interior of the house, Jess' voice reached out to them. "Mr. Miller? Mr. Miller? Are you back here?"

Thomas stepped away. "If you've got any common sense, you'll drop this." He raised his voice. "I'm in the kitchen."

"Ah, there you are. I'd heard you'd stopped by." She stuck out her hand in greeting and gave Devin a look that made his heart drop. Had she heard? "So what do you think? We're making good progress."

"So far I've seen some busted out walls, a ripped up kitchen, and a bunch of dirt. I guess that's what you call progress?"

Devin watched a muscle tense along her jaw but her smile didn't waver. "A project this size doesn't happen overnight. It takes time... and money. I assume escrow will have your next payment on Thursday, after the cement is poured?"

Thomas' eyes narrowed but his answer slithered out like the snake he was. "Of course. I understand the terms of the contract. You'll have your payment on time so the work can continue."

Jess was impressive. Devin had to give her that. She wasn't going to take any guff from his dad and wasn't going to give up any ground.

"Why don't you let me walk you through the project and explain what we're doing. Devin, I'll talk to you later." Jess started walking away giving Thomas no choice but to fall in beside her. "We'll be putting up a wall here and taking down this one so the kitchen flows into this space." Her voice faded as they progressed down the hall.

God she was magnificent. And he prayed she hadn't overheard anything he'd said to his father. The fact she wanted to talk to him made his knees feel like jelly. Sighing, he picked up his shovel, and dug the new plumbing trench lines. He'd know soon enough.

# Chapter
# Twenty-One

AT HER HOME THAT evening Jess paced the living room, periodically peering out the front window. She'd texted Devin that they needed to talk and he'd texted back saying he'd arrive shortly. She wanted to bang her head against the wall. What had she been thinking? That Devin was different? That she'd finally met a man she could trust? That she'd found a man who wouldn't lie to her and shut her out? That she was lovable for who she was and not what a man could get from her? She wasn't sure what Devin wanted, but he wanted something.

Love. How many kinds of fool was she destined to be? Experience should have warned her not to trust. First her college boyfriend dumping her for someone he thought could advance his career better than she could, then her most recent boyfriend trying to steal her clients. Unfortunately hormones had buried experience in a deep hole. She should have known it would worm its way back to the surface.

Devin's truck stopped at the curb and he stepped out carrying a pizza box and bunch of flowers. A smile momentarily touched her lips. It was just like him to make sure she ate. Anger gave that smile the kick in the butt it deserved propelled by what she'd overheard this afternoon. Devin was Thomas Miller's son? A man she disliked with an intensity that made her uncomfortable. The connection had never occurred to her. Devin had known that his father had basically stolen from her father?

She strode to the door and flung it open. He stood on her porch, hand raised to knock, his expression contrite and unsure. Her heart softened for the span of two heartbeats before her righteous anger again shoved its way to the front of her emotional lineup.

"Come in." She stepped back and pointed at the pizza box and flowers. "But don't think those are going to solve the problems I have with you right now." Pivoting quickly, she walked toward the kitchen. He could make his excuses later. At present she just wanted to seethe. She'd had to keep her cool this afternoon in front of the crew, but not now.

Devin set the box on the counter and opened its lid. The smell of hot pizza wafted through the kitchen. Her stomach growled. Okay, she was hungry. Silently, he retrieved two plates and glasses from the cupboard and iced tea from the refrigerator. She waited until they'd each placed slices of pizza on their plates.

"You're Thomas Miller's son?" Just saying the words ruined her appetite. "I didn't know he had any other children, except for the son who's a partner. Is Philip his name?"

"Yes. Philip. I wondered how much you'd heard." He sighed. "Yes, I'm his son, though he hasn't claimed parentage for almost twenty years." He pushed his plate away.

"All the times we talked about our parents and you never thought to mention who your father was? Why?" Her fingers itched to hurl something breakable at him.

"Honestly?"

"That would be nice for a change." She watched him flinch at the venom in her voice.

"I deserved that." His shoulders sagged and he dropped his head. "I assume you heard the part of the conversation about how my dad cheated the contractors he hired to work on his projects?"

Bile rose in her throat. "Yes, I did." Her heart thudded in her chest. "And I thought I heard my father's name mentioned." She shook her head. "Surely I misheard. You knew that my father was one of the people your father stole from?" Her fingers clutched the edge of the counter for support. "You didn't think it was worth sharing that information with me?"

Devin pressed his fingers into his temples and closed his eyes. When he opened them, she saw the raw pain there and almost—almost—felt sorry for him. "To answer your first question, I'm not exactly proud of being Thomas Miller's son."

White hot anger flashed through her body. With a supreme force of will, she pushed it back down. Jess made a checkmark in the air with her finger. "Check. Your dad's corrupt and you didn't want people to associate you with him. They could get the wrong idea." She pounded her chest with her palm. "But I'm not just anyone. I thought we had something special. That we could trust each other. Guess I was wrong on both counts." Like jumping into an icy lake, her breath caught in her chest and unshed tears clogged her throat. "I'd fallen in love with you."

He dug his fingers into his scalp and seemed to be having trouble drawing a deep breath. Finally he gently grasped her upper arms and gazed into her eyes with a passion she knew she would remember for the rest of her life.

"If I told you that you are the most important person in my life, would you believe me?" He released her, took two long steps away, and then faced her again. "I do trust you, and it was killing me not to tell you but all I had to go on was a phone conversation I overheard as a teenager. What good would it have done to tell you about my suspicions? I had no proof of anything. There was absolutely nothing either you or I could do to make things right for your dad."

She fisted her hands on her hips and challenged him. "So you decided that I didn't need to know who you are? You decided that you couldn't trust me to handle the truth? What? I'm too weak? I'm just a woman who needs to be protected? And for your information, my dad told me about his deal with your dad." Her heat level rose with each word until she was sure steam poured out of her ears.

Devin leaned his butt against the counter and crossed his arms over his chest. "Trust isn't the issue and no, I don't think you need my protection." His fingers moved nervously against his arm. "I didn't want to say anything because I was afraid if you knew, you'd reject me. Irrational, I know, but so many people in my life have rejected me for who I am. Your rejection would have broken me."

"Again, you made a decision that you couldn't talk to me about this. That I couldn't help you find the proof you needed?" Sadness sat like a massive boulder in her stomach taking up all the space and pressing against her diaphragm. Would she ever be able to draw a deep breath again?

"I'm sorry I didn't talk to you about all of this sooner. If it's any consolation, I planned to tell you everything when we went to Tahoe this weekend—and I learned in the last few days that what he's been up to goes way beyond swindling people."

"You do know that Tahoe is not happening now. Right?"

He ran a hand over his hair. "Yeah, I figured that. I'm guessing dinner with my sister tomorrow night is also off?"

"I think it would be a bit awkward meeting her right now."

He looked down at his feet. "Except for my sister, I've pretty much had to depend on myself to get by."

Jess had to strain to hear him.

He sighed again and continued to gaze at the floor. "Given my experience, trust wasn't something that came easily." Devin's eyes locked with hers. "I'm not trying to excuse myself. I should have trusted you. Returned the trust you'd given me. I returned to Sacramento to try and make things right. I joined your crew because your dad was the only person I knew who'd been cheated and hoped I could learn more. I hadn't planned to fall in love with you."

A sharp pain pierced her heart. He'd said the words out loud. He loved her but she still couldn't trust him. "What happens now? Are you going to try to get the people your dad cheated to press charges?" She held her breath. Her dad would hate for this part to become public.

"Other than your dad's, I don't have any names. Only rumors about who my dad might have cheated. Unless someone is willing to come forward and accuse him of wrong-doing, I think I'm at a dead end. Besides, as my dad pointed out this afternoon, it's probably all past the statute of limitations."

She swallowed past the lump in her throat. "You said your dad had been involved in other stuff. No more secrets. I want to hear it all."

He pushed away from the counter and stood in front of her, lightly running his hands up and down her arms. "I had no idea the can of worms I was opening when I started digging into my dad's business affairs. Why don't we sit down and I'll tell you everything?"

They sat at her small kitchen table and with each new revelation her heart dropped a little lower. By the time he finished an hour later, it had dropped into her feet.

"You do have quite a dilemma. Your dad really thought he was going to get away with all of this?" She sipped her tea hoping it would moisten her dry throat.

"He has so far." Devin blew a breath out between his lips. "I met with an attorney a few days ago to find out what kind of legal liability me and my siblings might face. After that I talked to Phil and Madison, and we're scheduled to meet with an attorney tomorrow evening to outline our next steps. Since our dad put our names on property titles in these holding companies and made us the owners of record on a number of businesses, moving forward is complicated." He hand formed a death grip on the glass he was holding. "Obviously we can't let this slide but we do want to protect ourselves as much as possible."

The cold fingers of dread clutched at Jess' throat. "You said you didn't know anything about the properties and businesses your names are on as principals? You had no idea business was being conducted in your names?"

"Yeah, that's right." His brows creased in confusion.

"Any idea what's going to happen to those properties that have been sold fraudulently?"

"I have no idea. Why?"

"Because the land we bought for our new office building had Philip's name on it as the principal owner under what I assume is one of these holding companies. The title came back clean but I'm wondering now if our deed's valid." She pinched the bridge of her nose. They'd finally found the perfect lot for their dream offices and the man who had ruined her father's business might put a big hole in her plans as well. *What a mess.* She felt like she had a case of food poisoning and might have to make a mad dash to the bathroom. She inhaled slowly and squared her shoulders. At least they had a heads up and could do damage control.

Devin's face paled. "Oh Jesus. How much more trouble is Dad going to cause? I'm so sorry you got tangled up in this too." He swiped a hand down his face. "I definitely suggest you talk to Ivy's high-powered attorney and do whatever he tells you to do. We'll figure a way out of this mess but my guess is that we'll all be talking to law enforcement real soon."

"You're right. I'm sure the courts will eventually sort things out about our ownership of the lot if it comes to that. We entered into a contract with Thomas in good faith and had no idea Philip wasn't the signatory on the notarized document." She placed her hand over his. "What's going to happen to your brother? I know he was close to your dad and is a partner in the firm."

He withdrew his hand and clasped them in front of him on the table. "With everything else that's come to light, he's stunned. Madison and I at least had the benefit of knowing Dad practiced dubious business deals for years. For Phil, it's all new. He's still trying to cope."

"How in the world do people dream up schemes like this?" Jess' mind felt as though she'd entered a cosmic void. The convoluted scenario barely made sense. "It boggles the mind."

"That it does." Devin cleared his throat. "I don't have any expectation that you've forgiven me, but do you think maybe someday you can?"

Jess got up and paced across the room and leaned against the cabinets. She needed space to breathe. "Once trust is broken, I can't just snap my fingers and restore it. You didn't believe in me enough to tell me what was going on. I'm going to need some time to absorb all this and what it might mean for Uniquely Yours. My partners and I have put our hearts and souls—not to mention our life savings—into the business. The thought of losing everything..." Dread's claws clutched at her stomach.

Devin stood and came to stand beside her. He leaned against the cabinets and and rested his hands behind him on the countertop. "Is there anything I can do to earn back your faith in me?"

"You need to be honest with me. No more secrets. And you need to give me time to believe you." She swallowed hard, and her hands trembled. "For now, especially until all this business with your father is concluded, we need to stop seeing each other. In the interim I'm going to assign you to Rollo's team."

The bleak expression on his face tore at her heart. "I'm hoping you'll eventually give me another chance." He brushed his fingers down her cheek and she flinched. "I can't tell you how much I'm going to miss you."

Blinking rapidly, she fought back the tears that threatened to fall. "You need to go now. I've got to let my partners know what's going on. Right now I can't see a second chance in our future."

"I'll go now." At the back door he paused. "I didn't mean to hurt you. I want you to know that I will do everything in my power to prove to you that I can be trusted and that I would trust you with my life." With that, he disappeared into the darkness.

Jess picked up her phone and texted each of the partners to find out when they could be available for an emergency conference call.

# Chapter Twenty-Two

JESS LOOKED AT THE somber faces gathered around the conference table. After last night's call, the partners had agreed to meet early this morning so Ivy could share what she'd learned after talking to their attorney.

"How bad is it?" Jess asked. "What did the attorney have to say?" She rubbed her arms and felt as though she was moving in slow motion.

Ivy pulled a file folder from her briefcase and glanced at her notes. "First, Caleb said we need to contact the Sacramento County District Attorney's Office, their Real Estate Fraud Division and make them aware of the situation. He's drafting a memo and collecting the documents we'll need to take with us. He gave me their phone number and suggested we call this morning and make an appointment." Her gaze swept the assembled partners. "Can everyone rearrange their schedules once we have a time?"

Everyone nodded their faces lined with worry.

"Nothing's more important than this," Victoria said with a hitch in her voice.

"What does this mean for the construction plans on the new office building?" Kaitlin asked.

"We should put a hold on plans to break ground until the DA has had a chance to investigate." Ivy thumbed through her notes. "Caleb said that as long the holding company didn't obtain the deed to the property fraudulently and the elusive Mr. John W. Bland, the Registered Agent who signed the documents, had the authority to sign for Philip or if he didn't, that Philip had agreed to the sale..." She paused and looked up. "You get the picture, it's going to take time to unravel all the threads and follow them to their origin."

"Well then, I guess the first order of business is for me to contact the Planning Department and put a hold on pulling the permits." Kaitlin opened her project management program on her laptop and scanned the work in the pipeline. "I'll get on that as soon as we finish here."

Jess turned to Ivy. "Didn't you say you have a couple of new properties in mind that might make good flips?"

"I do. Might as well keep busy while we wait this out," Ivy said. Her hands were clasped uncharacteristically tightly in front of her on the table.

"Are either of them auction properties so we'd need cash?" Jess gripped her own knees under the table.

"Nope, one is a foreclosure and the other an estate sale." Ivy exhaled and scrolled through her iPad. "The bank just announced that the foreclosure is available and the estate sale comes on the market at the end of the week."

Glancing over at Kaitlin, Jess asked, "Can we shift the funds we were going to use to get started on the new offices to the down payment on one of the new flips? What does our cash flow look like? We'll still have to make mortgage payments on the lot so everything looks normal."

Kaitlin tapped on her keyboard and studied her screen. "We're in good shape. We made the minimum down payment on the lot and financed the rest. Rollo's crew has wrapped up the Bridgeport Way flip and it's ready to sell." She tapped a few more keys. "I'll cancel the new construction loan for the office building, so we shouldn't have a problem getting a loan if we need it for a new flip." She reached over and patted Jess on the arm. "We planned for this," she rolled her eyes. "Well not this exactly, but we planned to make the mortgage payments on the lot and still have the cash flow we needed to buy a few more properties."

Jess blew out a breath and reviewed the construction schedule on her laptop. "All my crews are currently assigned to projects, although Rollo and his red team will finish the Jackson flip shortly after one of these new properties would close escrow. If we go for both of them, I'd have to hire on more people. I'm not sure I want to do that right now. Maybe we could do one?" She shrugged. "Thoughts?"

"Remember about a month ago I told you I had a potential new client who wanted a complete redesign on his home including landscaping?" Victoria didn't wait for confirmation. "He's ready to sign a contract and wants us to start right after the first of the year. With everything we have going and new inquiries coming in all the time, I say let's go for it." She leaned forward excitement punctuating her remarks. "We may have encountered a little setback but I say our balloon has plenty of room for more air." Her hand hit the table with a solid *thwack*. "We're strong and together we'll weather this storm."

"I'm game," Serenity said but her normally tan face looked pale.

"Count me in," added Kaitlin. Instead of her ready smile, her lips formed a thin line.

"The real estate market isn't showing signs of slowing any time soon. I can sell as many flips as we want to take on." Ivy closed her file folder. "Have we come to a decision?"

"I vote we call the District Attorney's Office and get that ball rolling, put a hold on the construction of our new office building, and then take a look at the new properties Ivy has in mind. Any discussion?" Jess glanced around the table.

Everyone shook their heads.

"I'd like to give Devin a heads up that we'll be talking to the District Attorney? Any objections?" Jess asked.

"I think I speak for the group," Serenity said. "They're victims too. It's the right thing to do and I'd be willing to bet that their attorney sends them to the District Attorney as well. In fact, you should probably pass along the contact info on our attorney. The two may want to compare notes. The more we cooperate, maybe the faster we can straighten everything out."

"Alright then," Jess stood, "I think we all have our marching orders. For now, let's keep this under our hats. No telling what Thomas Miller might do if he got wind of the shit getting ready to hit his fan. If anyone asks why we aren't starting construction on our new offices right away, tell them opportunities presented themselves that we didn't want to pass up so decided our offices could wait a while." She clenched her fists. "I'm pissed as hell that Thomas Miller has the money for the lot in his grubby hands, but at this point we're going to have to live with it and hope we get either the lot or our money when this is all over."

"I know we're all scared. We've got a lot of money on the line but let's try and make everything look business as usual to the outside world. I'll text everyone once I know when we can see the District Attorney. Keep your phones handy," Ivy said.

Just when she thought the dreams in both her personal and professional life would come true, the bird of fate dropped a load of poop on her head. She sighed and headed for her truck.

THIS HAD BEEN ONE of the longest weeks in Devin's life. Longer even than that first week of detox. He'd endured the irrational anxiety, the sweating, the tremors, the nausea, the stomach pain. Man he'd thought he was going to die. But this. His craving for Jess. He hadn't anticipated how much he would miss her—her touch, the sound of her voice, the sweet smell of the shampoo that clung to her hair, the taste of her lips. He sighed and dipped his paintbrush in the bucket beside him.

The transition to Rollo's red team had gone smoothly. He had no complaints there except that it separated him from Jess. Since he'd worked on the Jackson Street flip with Jess' green team, he knew the project and brought everyone up to speed. He'd been assigned to touch up painting today. All morning he'd been on his hands and knees working on the baseboards. Thank heavens, this was the last room.

Rollo had told him to help Serenity when he'd finished painting and Devin was more than ready to get outside for a while. Spotting Serenity adding landscaping to a border alongside the driveway, he wandered out to check in with her.

"Hey Serenity. I'm at your disposal." Inhaling the scent of the roses sitting nearby in pots, his body started to relax. "Looks nice. What can I do to help?"

"Grab a shovel and dig holes for these roses. Make the holes a little bigger round and deeper than the container and leave a small mound of dirt at the bottom of the hole." She picked up one of the containers, cradling it against her side, and walked over to him. "When it's in the ground the dirt should barely cover the soil the roots are in." She touched the soil next to the plant's stem. "Space the holes about two feet apart. Once you're done, I'll take care of the actual planting."

"You got it." He broke the ground with the shovel and started on the first hole. "How are all of you holding up?" he asked as he worked. "Sorry it put a crimp in building your new offices."

"We're doing as well as can be expected. Like you, we're in the legal limbo stage while the DA investigates and decides whether or not to prosecute. We won't know anything about the title to the lot for a while." She tilted one of the containers and manipulated it until the plant slid free. Setting it opposite the hole, she dusted her gloved hands. "What's that saying? Stay calm and carry on. What about you guys?"

"That about sums it up. At least one worry is off our backs. According to the DA, unless he turns up evidence showing any of us knew what was going on, we're considered victims and cooperating witnesses so we're out of legal jeopardy. Still lots left to deal with. Legal fees have put a dent in our in wallets. Madison has had to make room in her schedule for depositions and such. Luckily she can do most of that back east but may have to make trips out here if it goes to trial. Phil figures TLM Investments will fold and he'll need a new source of income, but he can't look for anything else right now or he might tip off dad." He picked up the plant and set it in the hole to check for depth. Satisfied, he started on the next hole.

"Has your brother come to terms with what your dad has done? Seems to me he's the one who's been hit the hardest. Jess said he'd do some discrete poking around to see what else he can uncover at work." She sprayed some water into the hole from the hose and tossed in a handful of what he assumed was some sort of nutrient.

Devin glanced over. "Jess filled you in on the whole sordid mess?"

"It's come up a time or two. Talking helps her process her feelings and she's definitely conflicted about the situation." Serenity knelt on the grass, gently hoisted the plant, and set it in place.

"Phil's adjusting and would eventually like to go into teaching." He shouldn't ask but he had to know. "How's Jess doing?" He dropped the shovel and placed the next plant in the hole. Pulling it out, he picked up his shovel and dug some more, then moved on to the next spot.

"Throwing herself into her work even more than usual. That's how she copes with uncertainty. She knows you guys didn't cause this mess and your lives have been turned upside down but that property has been her dream since we started Uniquely Yours. It frustrates her to have that future in jeopardy." Serenity rocked back on her heels and gazed up at him her expression questioning. "But that's not what you're really asking is it?"

He scrubbed his hand over the stubble on his chin. "No, I guess not. We fought and decided we shouldn't see each other for a while. I hadn't told her who I was or what I suspected my dad had done. She accused me of not trusting her."

"We all assumed something like that happened. Trust in a relationship is important to her." Serenity settled back onto her knees. "She appreciates that you've been calling her with updates. When she's passing along the information to the rest of us, it's one of the few times she smiles." Looking away, she focused her attention on the plant as she loosened its roots. "I know those smiles are because she's thinking about you. She misses you."

"I miss her too. I'm hoping she'll eventually forgive me." He stopped digging and leaned on his shovel. "I just don't know what to do to earn back her trust."

"I assume you're asking for advice?" She handed him the hose. "Add about six inches of water in the hole you just dug."

He did as instructed. "I'll take whatever insight you're willing to pass along. I'm hoping I haven't screwed this up beyond redemption."

"Jess has had a lifetime of her parents, especially her dad, not believing in her. Telling her she isn't capable of following her dream. Not trusting her to know what's best for her. Keeping things from her because—in her mind at least—they didn't believe she could handle it." Serenity moved over to the next hole. "It didn't help that in college she had a serious boyfriend who cheated on her. After that, she dated a fellow general contractor, and he tried to poach our clients. Her experience has reinforced the notion that trust should be doled out sparingly."

"I knew she had issues with her parents but guess I didn't understand how deep it went." He pulled a bandana from his back pocket and swiped it across the back of his neck. "She's never talked about any of her past relationships."

"Have you ever asked her? How much have you talked about your past life? Have you really opened up to her? Shared how you're feeling? Shared your dreams for your future?"

"I told her a little about my life after rehab but I guess I haven't really opened up." His gut danced with nervous jitters. "I think I was afraid that if she knew the real me—the guy who has no idea what his dreams are because that's something other people do—not a loser like me—she'd drop me."

"And there you have it. Not only did you keep secrets about who you are but you didn't trust her to understand." She stood and tapped him in the chest. "More important to our discussion, you don't have a lot of faith in yourself. You need to work on trusting yourself before you can begin to rebuild her trust in you."

He lifted his ball cap and ran a hand over his hair. "Got any ideas for how to go about that?"

"As a matter of fact, I do. I made some mistakes as a teenager that shook my confidence in myself and have spent years working on this issue." Regret lined her features before she shook it off and her usual calm demeanor returned. A rueful smile lifted the corner of her mouth. "I'm still working on a lot of this but I can offer some lessons I learned. First, be yourself, not the person you think everyone expects you to be."

He raised his brows. "I thought I was an open book."

Serenity rolled her eyes. "Keep telling yourself that, and you'll never climb out of the hole you've dug for yourself."

"Who am I pretending to be?" His lips compressed into a thin line.

"You said it yourself—a loser, a guy without dreams. That's not what I see, and I doubt that's what Jess sees." She angled her head. "Come on. Let's take a break."

Devin followed her to a shade tree in the middle of the front yard. Bags of bark were stacked under it. She sat and leaned her back against them. He reached into one of the ever-present coolers and passed her a bottle of water before settling himself beside her on the grass.

"Where's your crew?" he asked. "I was surprised to see you show up by yourself." He held the bottle against his cheek and let the ice slivers clinging to it melt against his skin.

"I have them installing a sprinkler system on another property." She nudged his shoulder with hers which made him smile. "I knew Bryan would assign a grunt to me so I wasn't worried I'd have to do everything myself."

"What's left to do?"

"Stalling?" She chuckled.

Heat rose up his neck. "Course not. Just curious is all."

"Finish planting those roses. Lay a drip line. Fill all the border areas, front and back, with this bark." She patted the stack of bags behind her. "Then my job is done."

He felt her gaze on him.

"Ready to face the music?" she asked.

Nodding, he plucked a blade of grass and smoothed it with his fingers.

"Buck up, pal. What I see is not bad." She placed her hand over his and stilled his fidgeting. He looked into her dark, brown eyes and his nerves stopped bouncing. "What I see is a man who seeks justice for the little guy. A man who is willing to stand up for what he thinks is right. A man works hard and is always ready to help one of his co-workers. I see a man who is a natural leader. I see a man who is strong and reliable. A man I'm proud to call my friend." She drew her hand back and then wrapped her arms around her bent knees. "I see a man with dreams he's simply been afraid to voice."

Devin ran his hands over his thighs. "You really see all that in me?"

"Yes, I do. The rest of my advice? Verbalize those dreams and set some doable goals to turn them into reality. Forgive yourself for whatever you perceive as your failings. Face the fact that you're human and we all screw up. Finally, recognize your strengths and build on them." She slapped his knee. "Easy Peasy."

"Once I have all that under control—and I may be old and grey before that happens—how do I earn back Jess' trust?" He stood and extended his hand to help Serenity up.

"For starters, you'll keep doing what you've been doing—keep her apprised of what's going on with the investigation. Once you've admitted to being the person you really are, not this fake guy, you can be honest about your feelings for her and your dreams for the future." They'd reached the driveway and she lifted one of the remaining containers of roses. "It's going to take time but I know she cares about you. Now let's get back to work so we can get out of here before dark."

Devin worked quietly beside her for the rest of the afternoon. Could he be the person Serenity described and would that be enough?

# Chapter
# Twenty-Three

TWO WEEKS WITHOUT Devin's touch. Devin's kiss. Devin's quiet, commanding presence. Two weeks that felt like an eternity. Jess had had no idea the void this lack of physical contact would create in her life. Sure, he called her with regular updates on the investigation and she treasured those moments. His voice made her heart beat faster and desire shoot down her spine. All that was great but no substitute for actually seeing him. Placing her hand in his. She sighed as she walked down the hallway heading for their regular weekly partner meeting.

Jess paused at the entrance to the conference room. Her eyes narrowed and she took an involuntary step backward. Why were all of the partners already here? Why had silence descended the moment she appeared in the doorway? Whatever they were up to, she didn't have the energy to deal with it.

"Hi Jess. Look, I already have your coffee ready, just the way you like it one sweetener packet and lots of cream... and a muffin too." Kaitlin pointed to the mug and plate neatly placed at the head of the table.

"I can see that." Oh yeah. This was a trap for sure but why? As far as she knew, she hadn't messed up and made her partners' lives miserable. That foot that had stepped backward had evidently gotten tangled in a lead boot and wasn't going anywhere without a great deal of effort. "Is this some sort of special occasion?"

"No. Not at all. We just know you've had a rough couple of weeks and wanted to do something nice for you." Kaitlin walked over to Jess and put her hands on her shoulders, gently leading her into the room and to her seat.

"Kaitlin, you should never play poker." Jess sat and took a sip of her coffee. "Okay ladies. What's up? From the half-eaten muffins in front of you and the nearly empty coffee cups, I'm going to hazard a guess and say you've been here a while."

"Jess, we love you." Victoria crossed her arms on the table and leaned forward. "But you really need to get your head out of your butt."

Jess did a double-take. "What? What are you talking about?"

Ivy glared at Victoria. "To put it a bit more delicately, you haven't been yourself lately and we're worried about you. We want to help."

"I'm fine." Heat flushed through Jess and her teeth clamped together. "Have I slacked off? Have I missed any deadlines? Am I not holding up my end of the business?"

"Anyone who looks like they're hosting Louis Vuitton bags under their eyes, has a problem," Victoria said. "And what kind of friends would we be if we didn't intervene?"

Serenity covered her eyes and shook her head.

"You'd be the kind of friends that trusted I can take care of myself," Jess spit out, clenching her hands so they wouldn't shake.

"Jess, we know you can take care of yourself. But it's not a sign of weakness to let others help you fight your battles." Serenity arched her brow and gave Jess a pointed look. "Both those we struggle with on the inside and those that come at us as external threats."

"We all appreciate and admire your independent streak," Ivy jumped in. "But we'd expect you to do everything you could to help if you saw any one of us wrestling with a problem." She tapped her manicured nail on the table. "Frankly, I'm hurt that you don't seem to expect the same level of support from us."

She looked around the table and the understanding and compassion emanating from each of them filled her heart to bursting. "I'm sorry. I didn't mean to shut you out but I'm not sure what you can do to make the situation better."

Kaitlin leaned over and hugged her. "Sometimes simply getting everything out in the open will help you find the path to resolution. We're all ready to be your sounding board." She sighed and sat back. "Every single one of us feels your pain. We know Devin hurt you and now you don't trust him. Tell us what's going on in your head."

"How do you know that's the problem and not the fact that we might lose the property for our new office building?" Jess asked her temper beginning to pulse at her temples.

Serenity raised her hand. "First, we're all worried about that but we're not losing weight and sleep over it. Only a man can do that to us." She shrugged. "And second, Devin talked to me about what happened between you." She pinched her lips together. "More to the point, he wants to know what he can do to win back your trust. He cares about you. To me that speaks volumes about his good sense and his character."

Jess narrowed her eyes. "What exactly did he tell you?" She glanced around the table again. "And by extension, told all of you?"

"That—with a little help from me—" Serenity placed her hand on her chest, "…he's seen the error of his ways. He knows he should have told you what was going on once he'd gotten to know you. Hiding behind the notion that he couldn't tell you because he didn't have proof that his dad had cheated your dad, was nothing more than cowardice on his part." Serenity clasped her hands on the table in front of her like a schoolmarm delivering a lecture. "Not surprisingly, given his background, he has trust issues of his own. He's working on that. The rest you need to ask him about."

"There's more?" Jess' body hummed with frustration. Wasn't it enough that he had hurt her by not trusting her?

"Have you ever pressed him to tell you more about his life? What he hopes for the future? How he feels about himself?" Serenity's tone was gentle.

"Of course I have. He always clams up." Jess felt the indignation rise like a mammoth wave pushing heat into her cheeks.

"I said *pressed*, not simply asked.

Jess wanted to squirm under Serenity's scrutiny.

"I thought as much. You let it pass. Why? Was he getting too close and you were afraid of getting hurt if you trusted him?" Serenity asked.

Ivy's calm voice hit her smack in the center of her soul. "I'm sorry sweetheart but trust is a two-way street. You have to get to a place where you're ready to let him in before you two can move forward. I know you've started down the path, but I'm guessing you need to finish squaring things with your dad in order to get your head on straight."

Jess felt sucker-punched. Her thoughts swirling as though caught in an emotional tornado. One that hadn't been on any forecast. She stood and stalked out of the room. She needed time to process. Glancing over her shoulder expecting to see shock or disapproval on her friends' faces at her unprofessional behavior, she was surprised to see encouragement instead. They got her. They really got her. She scrubbed her fists into her damp eyes and her sigh shuddered like a leaf in the wind. Looks like the first stop in her tour to reclaim her self-respect was to talk to her dad and let him know how he made her feel.

—ele—

"WELL LOOK WHAT THE cat dragged in. To what do I owe this unexpected visit?" Gerry took a swig from the beer bottle sitting on the end table beside his recliner. A baseball game flickered on the television.

Apparently her dad had returned to form. Insulting. Dismissive. Irritating. His post health scare frame of mind hadn't lasted long.

Darlene bustled into the room from the kitchen and hugged Jess. "It's always good to see you. Pay no attention to your father's bad mood." She put her hand beside her mouth. "His team's in a slump."

"I heard that." Gerry's voice lost its edge when he addressed his wife.

Her mother gave her the once over. "You look a little peaked, dear. Are you working too hard?"

Jess dug a smile out of her repertoire. "No Mom, I'm fine."

"Can I get you a beer or something?"

"No Mom. I just stopped by to talk to Dad for a while and then I need to get back to work."

"Well then, I'll leave you two. I'll be back in my craft room. Started work on a new quilt."

"That's great Mom. I'll come see it before I leave." Jess kissed her mom on the cheek.

"From the look on your face, I'll have to turn off my game?"

"Yeah Dad. You will." She'd heard the annoyance in his voice but too bad. He could just damn well pay attention to her for once. She was ready to stand up to him. "I'll keep it brief but I need to tell you something and then I'm hoping you'll answer some questions." Jess sat on the edge of the sofa.

Gerry took another long pull from his beer. "Okay. Shoot. Get whatever beef you've got with me off your chest."

If she'd been standing, Jess would have taken a step back from the impact. Is that where her inclination to distrust came from? Her dad always seemed to assume the worst about people's intentions. Had that rubbed off on her? Colored her view of people?

"It's not like that, Dad. I just wanted you to know you were right to be suspicious of TLM Investments. Thomas Miller is a bad actor through and through."

"Ah, ha. I knew it. He screwed you in that deal and you're coming to me with your tail between your legs." He sat forward in his recliner and slapped his knee.

217

She clamped her mouth shut and averted her gaze. Her dad was a piece of work. She rolled her eyes and shook her head. She may have inherited a sliver of his mistrustful nature but at least none of his meanness had ended up in her DNA.

"No Dad. He tried to pull a fast one on us but our company will be fine in the end." She clasped her hands in her lap. "What I want you to know is that we uncovered his illegal activities and have gone to the authorities. Thomas Miller is now under criminal investigation."

Her dad chortled. "About time. Can't say I'm surprised but why tell me?"

"First, you can't tell anyone he's under investigation. We don't want to tip him off."

"My lips are sealed." Gerry grinned and made a zipping motion across his lips. "Still, what's this got to do with me?" The suspicion had returned.

"You've let the bitterness over your business failure cloud your entire life. I'm hoping knowing that Thomas is finally going to pay for his dishonesty might make you feel vindicated. Not everyone is out to get you." Jess's hands trembled and she shoved them in her pockets.

Gerry slumped in his chair, deflated like a balloon. "So all of this is going to come out?"

"I don't think so. The DA is concentrating on Thomas' tax evasion schemes and potential money laundering." She brushed a hand over his balding head. "Dad, why didn't you tell me earlier the reason your business failed? Why couldn't you trust me with the truth when I was old enough to understand? Didn't you think I was strong enough to handle it?"

Her father did a double take, his expression one of incredulity. "What? Where would you get that idea?"

"Oh let me see." Sarcasm outlined each word. "*You're just a girl.* When I tried to mimic you on construction sites... *You can't do that. Construction's for boys. Why can't you be happy at home?* All my life I've lived with your put downs. Your disappointment in me."

"I get it. I was tough on you. Didn't want you to get hurt." Her father looked away and blew out a slow breath. "Did it ever occur to you that I hadn't told you earlier because I didn't want you to think of me as a failure? I wanted you to look up to me. I'd hoped no one would ever find out." He ran a hand over his face. "I was humiliated and saw no point in sharing that with the world."

"But Dad, I'm not the world. I'm your daughter." Something pinged in the back of her mind. Those words sounded familiar. "So all this time, it was ego and not a lack of confidence in me that kept you from telling me?"

Her father stood, picked up his beer, and walked over to the counter separating the kitchen from the family room. With his back to her he said, "Afraid so. Sending my business into a tailspin due to my poor judgement wasn't exactly my proudest moment." He cleared his throat. "I always wanted to be the best. Then you came along with all your success." He hung his head and his voice came out in a whisper. "I was jealous. Again, not my finest hour."

Jess walked over to stand beside her father. If she'd had a better relationship with her dad she might have hugged him but they weren't in that space yet. She hoped they'd get their someday. "Dad, we all make mistakes. I'm sorry you thought I'd think less of you if I knew. I wouldn't have. You're my dad and I love you no matter what." He turned his head and she saw moisture in his eyes. Maybe his mean-ness was really defensiveness. A way to shield himself from facing the disappointment he thought his life had become. Jess squeezed his shoulder. "Dad, I'm not judging you. My hope is that we can begin to appreciate each other and maybe be more the father and daughter we once were. Do you think that's possible?"

To Jess' utter amazement, he gave her an awkward hug. "I'd like to try."

Walking down the hall to see her mom, her steps felt lighter. She'd spent a lifetime being suspicious of people's motives. Her friends were right, she did need an attitude adjustment. From here on out, she'd make a conscious effort to trust. And Devin was at the top of her list.

# Chapter
# Twenty-Four

WITH A WIDE SMILE splitting her face and that feeling she got after she finished an energy drink, Jess stepped onto the Floral Road job site. The hum of power tools biting into wood was her favorite playlist and her feet wanted to dance to the rhythm. She'd pulled Devin back on to her team and couldn't wait to set eyes on him again. Her heart swelled at how much he'd been working to prove himself to her.

At least every other day he called to update her with any news he'd received from his attorney— fresh bits of evidence Phil had uncovered or that Ellen, TLM Investments' former CFO, had turned over. The DA had convened a Grand Jury and deposed her for more than thirty hours. Because the authorities had turned up documents that indicated money laundering was one of Thomas' crimes, the FBI had been called in to aid in the investigation.

Devin and each of his siblings had also appeared before investigators—though Madison had provided her testimony remotely in New Jersey—to document the forgery their father had committed without their knowledge. He'd heard through Ellen that other employees had been called to testify as well. While it would be months yet before the DA would decide whether or not to issue an indictment, signs pointed that direction.

Even the prospect of putting off construction on their new offices couldn't dampen her spirits. She had enough work to keep five crews busy for the foreseeable future. They could make do with their current office space for a few more years and if they had to find a new lot, they'd face that eventuality if it came. Nothing could dampen her spirits today.

She unzipped her hoody as she walked. Late October meant cool mornings but warm afternoons and today promised to be one of those delightful Indian Summer days. They'd completed the rough framing on the guest house and room additions and today were applying the sheathing and wrap to the exterior walls. That's where she'd find Devin. She waved at Jamal and Penny who were unloading rolls of insulation and stashing them in the garage before she disappeared around the corner of the house. The project was humming along and right on schedule. Thomas had paid each installment on time and hadn't made any demands that would hold up work—so far anyway—and she'd reached the point where she thought she could relax.

And there he was. Devin in all his studly glory. He'd already shed his sweatshirt and stripped down to his t-shirt. He and Ed were nailing the sheathing into place on the master bedroom addition. The *pop, pop, pop* of the nail gun punctuated the air as they worked. Devin stretched to reach the highest point of the piece he was attaching. She'd never tire of watching the play of muscles in his back, and his ass was a work of art.

He must have caught sight of her because he looked her way and grinned, hesitant but hopeful. Stepping away from his work, he lowered his safety goggles, and walked toward her. The heat in his eyes had her girly parts dancing a jig. Her hand wanted to slip into his but this was not the time or place.

"Looks like you guys are making good progress," she said.

"We are. Gonna do everything we can to keep this job on track. Seth and Hank have started putting sheathing on the guest house. Once Ed and I finish this section, we'll close in the kitchen and then help finish closing in the guest house."

She lowered her voice. "Can you come to my house after work today? I'd like to talk. Let's plan to go out to dinner afterward." The way his eyes lit up and the relief on his face made her want to wriggle like a puppy. His husky voice sealed the deal.

"You bet. Any time. Any place. I'll be there."

"Good. I'm going to check in with Jamal and Penny. Give them a hand installing the kitchen cabinets. I want to finish that job in the next few days. See you when you get over there?"

"Wild horses couldn't keep me away." They both started leaning toward each other, the urge for lips to meet strong. They caught themselves just in time and bounced back like they touched an electric fence. Jess shuffled away but not before she spotted Ed's grin. Heat crawled up her neck and she rolled her eyes.

An hour later Thomas found her in the kitchen unloading cabinet doors. Jamal and Penny were in the garage fetching another box of cabinets. The sound of nail guns and electric saws filled the background. Devin and Ed were installing the sheathing to the new exterior wall of the kitchen.

"What's this?" Thomas waved an invoice at her.

She held out her hand and he slapped the paper onto it. A quick glance told her it was the order for the cabinets from Quality Cabinets that she'd cancelled and replaced with cabinets from another vendor. "It's a canceled order." She handed the paper back to Thomas.

"But why was it canceled? The contract stated that you were to acquire all materials from specific companies." He waved his hand. "The cabinets you're installing aren't from one of the approved suppliers." He brought his face closer to hers and towered over her. Out of the corner of her eye she saw Devin step into the room. Thomas must have caught sight of him too because he glanced in that direction before returning his attention to Jess.

Jess stood her ground. "If you recall, the contract stated that we would use those suppliers unless we could find higher-quality materials for the same or lower price." She fisted her hands on her hips, narrowed her eyes, and leaned closer. Thomas took a step back. "The cabinets we're installing meet both criteria. I have the final say about what materials go into any project I'm in charge of."

"Well, I'm not satisfied and I'm not paying for this." Thomas eyed Devin. "You planning on coming to her rescue?" He nodded toward Devin. "You know he's my son?"

Devin crossed his arms on his chest and leaned his shoulder against the doorframe. "She knows and I'm here if she needs me but I suspect she can handle you all by herself. I trust her." He chuckled. "I'm just here to watch the show."

Jamal, Penny, and Ed had entered the kitchen from the other side and their heads swiveled toward Devin.

Thomas sneered. "I'm surprised he acknowledged the fact. He seems to think I'm the devil incarnate."

"Actually, it was more like full disclosure. Doesn't matter to me whose son he is. I'm only impressed by the quality of his work." Out of the corner of her eye she saw the thumbs up his fellow crew members gave Devin. A bubble of warmth spread through her chest.

"Now back to the contract," Jess said. "You have every right to withhold payment. Just remember we have a binding arbitration agreement and if they rule against you, you'll be responsible for all work-stoppage costs, including the wages of my crew." She shrugged. "If you want to proceed with your complaint, go ahead. I'm sure my crew won't mind a few days off."

Thomas sputtered. "We'll see about that." Turing on his heel, he stormed out of the room.

Jess grinned at the high-fives her crew exchanged. "Okay everyone. Show's over. Get back to work."

THEY'D AGREED TO GIVE themselves time to shower and change after work before meeting a Jess' house. She sat on the bottom step of the stairs and her gaze slowly swept the foyer and the adjacent rooms. So many memories... good memories... of her and Devin here.

A knock at the door and she moistened her lips. He was here, and she hoped they could find their way clear to move into a shared future. She knew now that's what she wanted—a forever with Devin. Standing, she moved to the door, nerves jangling through her body like fireworks.

He held a supermarket bouquet of autumn flowers in his hand. His dark hair was still damp and brushed back from his forehead and beginning to form loose curls about his shoulders. She loved this man.

"Come on in."

He handed her the flowers.

She buried her nose in them. "They're beautiful." He followed her as she headed to the kitchen for a vase. Once the flowers were taken care of she grabbed his shirt and pulled him down for a deep, satisfying kiss. Her sigh mingled with his. "I needed that." She felt his smile against her lips.

"I needed that about two weeks ago and every day in between," he said. Devin started to say something else and she placed a finger against his lips.

Taking his hand, Jess led him back into the foyer. Settling herself on the bottom step she patted the space beside her. She hadn't wanted to hold this conversation anyplace as formal as the living room or with a table between them in the kitchen. She needed to feel his heat. She needed their bodies to touch. Facing him, their knees bumped.

"I understand why you didn't share who you were and why you returned to Sacramento..." He inhaled and she placed her hand on his chest. "I'm sorry you didn't feel comfortable telling me. I'm also sorry I didn't send out the right signals. I didn't open up to you entirely either. Trust has never come easily to either of us. People have let us down. Our life experience has molded us but I don't want it to define us as individuals or a couple."

Devin captured her hand and brought it to his lips. "I want that too, but I don't want to let you down. Trusting and having people depend on me is new to me. It may take a while to get used to the experience and believe in myself. I'm working on it but I'm asking for your patience."

"It's been pointed out to me recently, that I have a few things to work on too. I've also learned a few things about myself in the last few weeks." She paused to collect her thoughts and was pleased that Devin knew her well enough to wait. "I had a talk with my dad yesterday. I always thought I was this big disappointment in his eyes. Turns out I was wrong. He was disappointed in himself, but his bitterness and negativity influenced the way I expected people to treat me. I didn't trust people's motives. I don't want to be that person anymore. I hope you'll be patient with me as well." She curled her fingers in his. "While I appreciate having others respect what I do and what I've made of myself, I know now that I'm enough all by myself. No matter what happens, I can take care of myself, but life is so much better when I let people in. I've experienced that with my friends. They've made my life so much more complete but something's missing. When you showed up and filled my heart, I discovered that what was missing was you."

Devin framed her face in his hands and pulled her in for a kiss. Every part of her wanted to melt into him.

"I've been doing some soul-searching as well. You're so right about the trusting not coming easy. However, a wise woman told me that I can't trust others until I begin trusting myself." His fingers tangled in her hair. "I was afraid if you knew the real me, the me I thought I was, that you'd reject me—like so many other people in my life had."

She reached over and stroked the hair away from his face. Touching him was a balm to her soul.

He smiled and captured her hands between his. "Don't distract me or I'll never get this out." He inhaled deeply. "Turns out I'm not that person. I'd never given myself permission to dream about my future because I thought I was a loser. I didn't deserve to expect anything better than what I had. My sister started the turn-around by getting me into rehab, but working with you and your crew showed me, I have things to offer."

"Oh Devin." She traced the line of his jaw with her fingers. "I hope you see what I see. A man who's strong and dependable and loving. The man I want as my life partner."

His grin lit up the room. "That's good because I've given myself permission to dream, to envision a future. I want the kind of relationship I never had growing up—someone to hold hands with, to share life's little moments with, to cuddle with on the sofa. I want to settle down. I want to have a family. I want you. A life with you. A forever with you. I want to create a home with you. A place where we'll laugh, and love, and grow old together. What do you say? Are you ready to share my dream?"

"I was looking around this place before you arrived and realized that this is simply a house without you in it. With you, it's a home. You're the home I've searched for all my life."

"I'm going to take that as a yes."

"Oh yes. You are my heart and my home."

*Three months later.*

HAND IN HAND, Devin and Jess walked down the courthouse steps. Philip and Shelly, who cradled their newborn son in her arms, walked beside them. Madison and her fiancé, Jonas, brought up the rear. Serenity, Ivy, Victoria, and Kaitlin waited for them on the sidewalk below. They'd all just witnessed Thomas' arraignment. While the trial was months off, the process for bringing Devin's father to justice had begun.

Jess squeezed Devin's hand. "You okay? I know you haven't been on good terms with your dad for a long time, but it's still got to be hard to watch his downfall."

"It is. Bittersweet really." He bent and his lips feathered against her temple sending a fresh wave of sparks down her spine. "Makes me think about all the 'what ifs'. If he'd made other choices, if I'd made other choices, how different would our lives might have been."

"But everything that has happened in our lives has brought us to this point." She glanced down at the gold band on the fourth finger of her left hand. They'd gone to the courthouse just before Christmas, and in the presence of a small group of family and friends, had gotten married. "I'm not complaining."

They'd reached the bottom step and Devin paused. Framing her face between his hands, he kissed her solidly on the lips. "Neither am I." He shook his head. "Can't believe I'm starting back to college in a few weeks to study construction management. In a few years, I'll have my general contractor license."

She loved the look of bemusement on his face. As though he wanted to pinch himself. "And when you do get your license, you'll share my partnership position in Uniquely Yours."

"I would have been happy continuing as an employee but am grateful for the trust all of you have put in me." He smiled at each of the partners and they beamed back at him.

Jess grinned at her friends. "We talked about it, and it only made sense. One of these days you and I will want to start a family, which will make it difficult for me to run the construction side of things for a while." She patted his arm and relished the proud tilt to his lips that brought out his dimples. "You're our backup plan. Besides, if the company continues to grow the way it has, I won't be able to handle all the work by myself."

He glanced at the sky and inhaled. "There have been a lot of changes in our lives." He put his hand at the small of her back and steered her toward the parking garage. "Good changes."

"I, for one, am looking forward to what this year—and all our future years together—will bring."

*THANK YOU FOR READING* WELCOME HOME. *I hope you enjoyed Jess and Devin's story as much as I enjoyed writing it. If you did, I would greatly appreciate you leaving a review on Amazon or the review site of your choice. Reviews are much appreciated and crucial for any author. A line or two about your experience can make a huge difference in attracting other readers. Click here to leave your review*

*IF YOU ENJOYED WELCOME HOME, then don't miss this next book in the Hearts & Home series!*

Serenity Gagliardi is up next in a second chance at romance story. Her past is riddled with secrets—secrets that concern her high school and college sweetheart and could destroy the love they once shared. No longer able to play the sport he loves at a professional level, Travis Southwick's future is shrouded in uncertainty. Now he's back in town and would like to rekindle the romance with the woman he's never been able to get out of his heart. Can love blossom when the past and present collide?

*A beautiful, well told story with likable characters that you cheer on with a storyline that keeps you interested to the end Can't wait for the next book in the series. ~ Amazon Reviewer*

Find out by clicking here and picking up your copy of SERENITY'S GARDEN. The book is also available in Kindle Unlimited. Want to know more? Read the book blurb below.

—— *ele* ——

**BOOK BLURB**

*Her past is riddled with secrets. His future is shrouded in uncertainty. Can love blossom when the past and present collide?*

Landscape designer Serenity Gagliardi is a successful businesswoman. Along with four friends, she rejuvenates neglected properties and takes them from forgotten to fabulous. But her heart hides a secret that she's buried in the pursuit of a full and happy life. After her first and only love reappears, old yearnings flame—igniting the fear she may lose the one thing she prizes above all else...

Pro soccer player Travis Southwick has lived a charmed life in the spotlight, until an injury forces him to leave the game he loves. Facing an uncertain future, he returns home to care for his recently widowed mother. Thrust into the path of his childhood sweetheart, the only woman he ever loved, Travis finds his desire for her burns as hot as ever. But Serenity was the one who abandoned their plans for a life together.

Serenity's secret once revealed, forces Travis to face new challenges and build new dreams. Is there a chance they can open their hearts to love a second time? Beyond the fear and doubt stems hope that the truth is a seed, one that can grow into love, coming at last to full bloom...

*Serenity's Garden* is the second book in the captivating Hearts & Home contemporary romance series. Read an excerpt below.

Excerpt from Serenity's Garden (*Travis learns that Reanna is his daughter*)

With a hand on her daughter's back, Serenity guided Reanna to her truck. He felt the vein pulse at his temple, and his fingernails bit into his palm. Never in a million years would he have thought that Serenity could betray him like this.

Coach Janice cleared her throat, and he forced himself to concentrate on the children in front of him. "We'll start with some warm-up drills. Who wants to help set out the cones?" All twelve players raised their hands, eager to help. "Perfect. Each of you get a cone out of the bag and follow me. I'll show you where to put them." The girls dashed to the canvas bag with the bright orange cones, and Travis slung the mesh bag with the balls over his shoulder. When everyone was ready, he led the way to the middle of the field.

After they had the cones equally spaced in two lines, he emptied the sack with the balls. Travis held up his hand to keep the girls from racing forward and grabbing a ball. "How many of you have done ball handling drills?" Every hand when up except for one little girl's, the one he'd dubbed shy Molly. "Great. You'll each take a ball and dribble it down one side of the cones, cross to the second line of cones, and then return to the start. Coach Janice will demonstrate." Once she'd run through the drill, Travis continued. "Remember to keep the ball close to your body, Don't let it get too far ahead of you and use both feet. Reanna, would you start us off?"

"Yes, Mr. ..." Reanna looked confused.

Travis smiled. "Just call me Coach." He liked the sound of that. Wasn't sure he would but found that he did.

"Yes, Coach." He admired the way she marched to the pile of balls and then took her place at the starting point. His eyes narrowed and he watched her more closely, then shook his head, not sure what thought was trying to move from his subconscious.

"The rest of you line up behind Reanna. When she passes the second cone, then the next in line will start. Coach Janice will help you." As the other girls lined up, he crouched in front of Molly. "Is this your first time playing soccer?"

She stared at the ground, and her dark pigtails bounced as she nodded.

"I'm hoping you'll be my partner and help me practice my drills. Would you like that?"

Again, the pigtails bobbed but with more vigor this time. She looked up and smiled, and Travis was glad Ham had talked him into coaching. These girls had already stolen his heart.

While he worked with Molly, he kept an eye on the other players. Occasionally he'd pause to call out instructions or motion Coach Janice to help one of the girls with her technique. Several of the girls held a lot of promise, but he wholeheartedly supported the league's emphasis that girls of all levels of proficiency should play on each team. The focus was on balance and not creating superteams.

AYSO had had the same policy when he'd played as a kid. It wasn't until he'd hit high school and played on the varsity team that he'd come to understand how much his earlier experience with players of mixed skill levels had shaped his outlook. He learned stars were nothing without their teammates. Lifting up the weakest player lifted them all and made him both a better person and better player. He wanted these kids to learn the same lessons.

"Now we're going to switch to passing drills. Reanna, will you partner with Molly?" Reanna's face fell for a second, and she glanced at Leah who Travis had already surmised was her friend.

Travis opened his mouth to pair Molly with someone else when a grin spread across Reanna's face and she walked over to the other girl and took her hand. "Come on, Molly. I'll show you how to do the drills. It'll be fun. You did really good with the dribbling."

Travis felt his heart expand even more and was touched at how Reanna took Molly under her wing. Ham was right. Travis would get more out of this experience than he could possibly give the girls. This was what the game was all about.

After they'd completed the drills, Travis talked briefly about the basic roles of the various positions and a rudimentary recap of the rules. He supported the league's focus on developing the kids' skills. Giving them the confidence to enjoy the game and play to the best of their abilities without feeling like they weren't good enough. He wanted to be the kind of coach the AYSO sought—positive, patient, and inspiring. Once he finished his talk, Travis divided them into two teams so they could scrimmage.

Standing on the sidelines, watching the girls' determination to master the skills he endeavored to pass on, a satisfied warmth suffused his body. It did his heart good to watch them help and encourage each other. He'd become so accustomed to the hyper-competitiveness of the professional players that he'd forgotten the sheer joy of playing just to play.

Arms crossed, he inclined his head toward Coach Janice who was standing beside him. "I'd say we have a great group of girls. Should be an exciting season."

"I'm looking forward to it. Thank you, by the way, for helping Molly. She's my daughter and never played soccer before. We're new to the area, and I hoped being on a team would be a good way for her to make some friends. I'm sure you've noticed, she's shy."

"You're welcome." He nodded at the field. "She seems to be fitting in nicely. Have you coached before?"

"No, but I thought Molly might feel more comfortable if she had a familiar face around."

He noticed out of the corner of his eye that parents were beginning to arrive to pick up their daughters. His heart beat faster when he spotted Serenity chatting with the other parents. He put the whistle in his mouth and signaled for play to halt. When the girls looked his direction, he waved them in. They dashed toward him, circling him. Those in the inner ring hugged his legs. The emotions clogging his throat nearly floored him. He patted the backs of the ones he could reach.

"Good practice, ladies. I'll see you all again on Thursday afternoon and again on Saturday morning. Now go get your snacks." Excited chatter and giggles drifted back to him as the girls raced to the snack station.

Travis headed toward the group of parents standing on the sidelines. Part of the gig was being available for questions and reassuring them that their daughters were doing well. He also hoped for a minute alone with Serenity. With luck he could talk her into dinner and a movie in the next few days. He managed to shake hands with everyone, making sure he got to Serenity last. Parents started drifting away after their daughters had collected their snacks.

Reanna dashed up and threw her arms around Serenity's waist. "Mom. Coach Travis is great and so was practice. I can hardly wait until Thursday."

His gaze flicked back and forth between mother and daughter. Hugh boulders rumbled and crashed against his skull. What was it his brain was trying to tell him? "You've got a great little soccer player there. Must have gotten that from her dad." The color drained from Serenity's face.

"Well, she definitely didn't get it from me." Her smile wobbled, and then she looked down at the ground. Her fingers fidgeted with the straps on her backpack. "We need to be going. Reanna has homework to do." She took her daughter's hand. "Come on, sweetheart. We should let Coach Travis get on with his work."

"Shouldn't we stay and help?" Reanna asked.

"Um..." Serenity looked uneasy.

His eyes narrowed and he studied Reanna. Hair like his. Eyes like his mother's. She was his daughter. The earth shifted, and then it felt like the ground opened beneath him and he was falling. His stomach lodged in his throat. He couldn't breathe. Is this how drowning felt?

"I could use some help. Reanna, why don't you take this bag and go collect the balls. I'd like to have a word with your mom." When Serenity made a move to follow her daughter, Travis placed a restraining hand on her arm. "Oh no, you don't."

The girl scampered off and once she was safely out of earshot, Travis let the shock pour out of him. "Reanna is my daughter, isn't she?"

Serenity nodded.

"How could you keep something like that from me?" When she started to speak, he held up his hand. "Now is not the time nor place, but you and I need to talk. Today. I'm sure you can find someone to watch Reanna."

"But..."

237

He cut her off as Reanna approached, dragging the bag of balls. "Today, Serenity. I'll see you at my place in a few hours." With that he released her and ran a hand over his hair. "Go, before I say something I shouldn't."

Striding over to Reanna, he took the bag from her and slung it over his shoulder. "Thank you for helping. I'm glad you're on my team."

She threw her arms around his waist and buried her head in his stomach. "I'm so glad you're my coach. It's going to be the best year ever." He swallowed past the emotion that clogged his throat then leveled a hard stare at Serenity over the child's head. "Go with your mom now, and I'll see you at practice on Thursday."

*Don't miss the second book in this exciting new series by Bonnie Phelps. Get your copy of SERENITY'S GARDEN today! The book is also available in Kindle Unlimited.*

# Also By

Serenity's Garden: A Hearts & Home Novel Book 2

*Matchmaking Ghosts*

More Than Pretty: Matchmaking Ghosts Book 1

# About Author

Rumor has it that Bonnie began telling stories at a very early age. Photos exist of the author toddling around the corner of the house covered in mud babbling about magic rabbits leading her through the garden. Her parents were amused – until they discovered she had also walked across the newly poured cement patio – which only added fuel to the fire of her passion for writing. From then on, her active imagination continued to churn out plots and character sketches always wondering how different people would behave in similar situations.

Bonnie used her writing skills throughout her professional life as a fundraising and communication executive for several nonprofits. She enjoyed the chance to tell and share the story of worthy organizations. In the late 1980s, Bonnie authored a syndicated column in several California newspapers in which she shared the experiences and misadventures of life as a wife and mother. The jury is out on whether or not her children always appreciated her candor. Because Bonnie has romance in her soul, she also worked as a Wedding Planner for several years. Absolutely loved it!! She craves anything sweet, revels in any chance to travel, and is addicted to tracing her family's roots. A native Californian, the author lives in Northern California with her husband.

Learn more about Bonnie and her books at her website: Bonnie Phelps Author

Have a question or comment? Send Bonnie an email at: bonnie@bonniephelpsauthor.com

SIGN UP FOR MY NEWSLETTER for monthly updates and exclusive behind-the-scenes news, writing updates, my favorite recipes, books I've read and recommend, and occasional drawings for books or hand-knit scarves.

Connect with Bonnie:

Facebook

# Acknowledgments

Thank you to my critique partners – Elsa and Dawn – for reading multiple first drafts and helping fine tune my manuscript. I take each and every suggestion to heart. Thank you also to my fellow Romance Writers of America friends and colleagues, especially my Yosemite Romance Writer and Sacramento Valley Rose Chapter mates. Your friendship and well-aimed head slaps makes each book I write better. A special thank you to my content editor, Anna J. Stewart. You rock! Your guidance takes my writing to new heights. Finally, thank you to my proofreader, Dayna Hart of Hart to Heart Editing for polishing my manuscript and making it print ready.

Printed in Great Britain
by Amazon

17305559R00144